The Loved One

The Loved One
Edited & Compiled by Sanyogita Bharadwaj
Print Edition

First Published in India in 2021
Inkfeathers Publishing
New Delhi 110095

www.inkfeathers.com

The Loved One

Edited & Compiled by

Sanyogita Bharadwaj

Inkfeathers Publishing

DISCLAIMER

The anthology "The Loved One" is a collection of 20 stories by 19 authors who belong to different parts of the globe. The anthology editor and the publisher have edited the content provided by the co-authors to enhance the experience for readers and make it free of plagiarism as much as possible. Unless otherwise indicated, all the names, characters, objects, businesses, places, events, incidents- whether physical/non-physical, real/unreal, tangible/ intangible in whatsoever description used in this book are either the product of the author's imagination or used in a fictitious manner. Any resemblance to actual persons, objects, entities, living or dead, or actual events is purely coincidental. The stories published in this book are solely owned by their respective authors and are no way intended to hurt anyone's religious, political, spiritual, brand, personal or fanatic beliefs and/or faith, whatsoever.

In case, any sort of plagiarism is detected in the stories within this anthology or in case of any complaints or grievances or objections, neither the anthology editor, nor the publisher are to be held responsible for any such claims. The author(s) who holds the rights to the story/stories, shall be held responsible, whatsoever.

CO-AUTHORED BY

Saranya Dhandapani | Anurag Mallick | Parasa Meghana | Laasya Pemmaraju | Rosalind Princess Reshma | Raga Lahari | Madhurya Kommuri | Shagabandi Mmanish | Shubha Pai | Anshika Prem Chhatani | Johnny Pasapala | Aishwarya K| Mansi Gupta| Debjyoti Das | Elizabeth Caroline Palaparthi | Praneetha Sivalenka | Adyasha Pattnaik | Bhavya Rao | Dragon Slayer

CONTENTS

ABOUT THE EDITOR

Sanyogita Bharadwaj

Sanyogita Bharadwaj is a twenty-one-year-old who hails from Hyderabad. She is currently pursuing her Bachelor's in Psychology, Journalism and Literature from Villa Marie Degree College for Women. Some of her work that has been published is Hope & Beyond, As I Learnt to Fly and Musings of the Soul. Sanyogita was first published in the romance anthology, The Love I know where she won the competition and bagged herself a place in the anthology lead by renowned Indian Author, Geetika Saigal. She likes to call herself an occasional writer and a voracious reader. Her life revolves around books, art, and music. She believes books are the fuel to an active imagination. One can learn from books that what isn't taught in institutions. Also, one can go to a million places and meet many people through a book is what she thinks. She aspires to learn as much as one can in life from life, be it different languages, art, dance form or anything. Literally every time life would like to teach her a new thing, she says she'd be an obedient disciple to life. She also likes to cook occasionally. She believes knowledge and experience is the key to everything. She aspires to be a Psychologist. 'With love and lil' more love' is what she lives by.

PREFACE

How many times have we heard the word 'Love'? And how somehow most of us associate it with the romantic kind. But love never had boundaries neither was it ever bound just to romance. Love is beyond. Love is an emotion one can have for anyone irrespective of the relationship one shares. At times love is when your mother feeds you that extra morsel of rice, when your father bonds with you over a cricket match, when your sibling agrees to share his/her ice cream tub with you because you had a long day, when a friend makes you feel like a long lost sibling, when the post man's cycle's bell brings or the milk vendor's arrival bring a wide smile on your face, or a simple conversation with someone at the bus stop, at times even you making a cup of coffee for yourself because self-love is important too, yes you read it right! Not just romance but love is not just bound to blood as well. Love and affection is everywhere, where you express it and see it.

Every story here reminds you of a bond in your life you truly cherish. Our bonds with people around us might be bitter-sweet, but on bitter days it's love that bonds you again with the person. As though when the light of affection takes away all the bitterness in words and the dark in the bond fades away just like that. On the coldest and lowest days of life wraps everyone longs to be wrapped in the warmth of this blanket called, 'Love'. Life for sure is like a roller coaster ride where you don't know what's ahead, but you know that someone will always hold your hand and also have the thrill of it. Similarly, throughout life, on different paths of life, some or the other loved one always holds our hand and make sure we don't ride alone vice versa.

The sole motive of 'The Loved One' is to show you journeys of love beyond romance and how one ends up bonding even with a stranger apart from known people only to develop a bond of unconditional love and affection.

The Loved One

1

She's A Fantasy

by Saranya Dhandapani

Opposite poles attract each other' is not only for magnets but also for people. I have a sister, and her name is Shakthi. Guess what Shakthi means in the Tamil language? Shakthi means "The Power." My parents gave her the name without any expectation that she would become like one in the future. Though I hate her for providing me hard times, she is one tough woman.

When I was born three years after her, I took over all her beautiful toys and dresses. As she was too young to pull a fight with me, she stayed calm. She was a reticent, balanced child at a young age. But I was just the opposite. All the toys she has been protecting for three years, I broke them in only thirty days and asked for more toys. She wasn't reacting to any of my playful behaviours. Maybe that's why my parents loved having her around than me. They got tired of me all the time. I was so hard to control. On the other hand, my sister was such a beautiful, well-behaved child.

During my childhood, as I was always roaming around the streets and having fun, I didn't play with her more. We had spent most of our childhood in that place only. When I turned four, my parents bought a new house, and we moved there.

That's when I and my sister started coming closer. As we were new to the place and were yet to make new friends, we started enjoying each other's company for the first time.

There were many new-born babies and children in our area. We both love children and would like to play with them. But Shakthi never allowed me to carry any baby whenever I was with her. She would ask me to hold the baby for two minutes; later, she would come up with silly reasons and take them from me. I was the most disappointed younger sister in the world whenever she did something like this to me.

On weekends, I always wanted to play with my medical kit and kitchen set toys in the afternoon because mom didn't allow us to go outdoors at noon. Shakthi would play with me only If I gave her the toys which she wanted. I often got confused about who is the younger one here. Because my friends used to tell me stories like their brother gave this, their sister gifted their old toys. But in my case, it was just the opposite. She wasn't the typical elder sister, after all. Though I hated her for taking away my favourite toys, I had no choice but to play with her.

We studied in the same school. Whenever my friends gave me any snacks which I knew my sister would like, I went to her class and gave it to her in my leisure time, and she did the same too. That was the only reason for us to communicate in our school.

I used to watch TV series and movies a lot. But Shakthi loved songs only. She was a beautiful singer too. Like every other sibling, we had our own "this is my turn" fight for remote and TV times. I started listening to Carnatic music because of her. Days passed with all our little fights and arguments.

Her Board exams were coming soon, she wasn't so serious about them, and she was enjoying her last few days in school. That surprised me because I was the type of person who took everything seriously, worked hard, and wanted everything to be perfect. She was precisely the opposite of me. She used to take things lightly and enjoyed every moment in her life as if it were her last day on Earth. That's something I learned from her when I grew up.

I studied the ninth standard when Shakthi completed high school, and she was all set to start college. When the whole family asked her to study computer science or Engineering, she stood up for herself and told her that she would study English Literature. Everyone tried to convince her in every possible way, but she was not convinced and studied Literature. Whenever I think of how she stood up for her dreams, I regret myself for not fighting enough for what I wanted and for choosing Engineering over Journalism. I never had enough guts to fight for what I wanted back then.

She was all set to move to a new city for her college. I went along with my dad to drop her at the bus stop. I started crying halfway on the road, and she cried too. But later, I enjoyed being alone at home. I didn't have to fight for the remote anymore; I could hold any babies without her disturbance. All that fun lasted for two weeks; then, I started missing her. I was sitting on the stairs and was crying silently.

Whenever she came for holidays, I listened to her stories, took her literature books, and started reading Literature for the first time. Over time, our bond became more powerful every day. It didn't mean that we stopped fighting. We had our meaningless fights as always, but the love was so more potent than those. She was done with under graduation and came back home for her Post Graduation.

In our early 20's, we both looked so similar, and everyone who saw us together would go like, "Hey, wait! Are you, twins?" Even Google got confused and asked, "Same or different person?" I was happy with the fact that we had some similarities in our appearance because we had nothing in common. She was the one who introduced me to makeup, eyeliners, kajal, and lip shades. Her Post Graduation and my Under-Graduation days started together.

We both shared accessories, and we had all the fun. Shakthi was this bold girl who would even slap a guy if he flirted or misbehaved with any of us. When I was a teen, she taught me to stand up for what I want, and she taught me a few swear words to use in case of emergency. She wasn't the "advising" type of sister. She tells things randomly on a walk or while watching a movie. She somehow got to know everything I do as if she were monitoring me on a camera. She never scolded right away after knowing things. She had the strange kind of patience and dropped stuff at the oddest of times. That is one thing I was always afraid of Shakthi. "Expect the unexpected" is not only Micromax's tagline but also hers.

The harder I try to hide things from her, the easier she finds them. So, I started telling her everything: my crush, my anxiety, anticipation, and fear. But she knew it all already. I felt so comfortable and found myself at peace after telling her everything. I didn't have any trouble in my teenage, because Shakthi had it all covered. I never worried about not having an elder brother because I got my "Shakthi." She is so friendly and can get along with anyone in less than a minute. I was just the opposite of her. My friends used to visit my home not to spend time with me, but with my sister. She was the most jovial and happening person I have ever known. I started admiring her a lot and felt so lucky to have a sister like her.

She completed her Post-graduation and all set for her wedding. Things were happening so fast, and I didn't even realize that I was going to miss her. It was that time of the night I told her that I love her so much and would miss her annoying me while sleeping. It was that time of the night when we kept our phones apart and hugged each other tighter. It was that time of the night when I realized that I have the most beautiful sister. It was that time of the night when we walked down the memory lane together. It was that time of the night when I promised her, I would be more responsible. Because the very next day, she got married and moved to a new city.

I cried a river on her marriage. It is weird to say that I can't live without her, but I can never even imagine my life without her. Days passed, and we often met. Nothing has changed after her marriage. We were the same annoying sisters. I completed my Engineering, and like most of the Engineers, I struggled a lot for my first job. My family started advising me to prepare for government exams and bank exams. Even though I didn't like Engineering when I joined; slowly, I developed a passion for it and learned many. So, I didn't want to give up. Only because of her encouragement, I persistently tried and cracked the interview of the famous IT Company. After getting the result, I went to meet her, and we both hugged in tears. It was Shakthi who strongly believed in me when no one else did. It was she who always told me that I deserve the best. It was she who believed in my hard work more than me.

I got a job and moved to Bangalore. I never stayed away from home, and everything was a brand-new experience for me. The long-distance relationship brought Shakthi and me even closer. But I hardly told her that I missed her a lot. I visited her whenever I had holidays, she used to cook all my favourite food in an hour just to put that big smile on my face. Life was so good.

A few months later, I got a call from her husband that she was admitted to the hospital. I was reminiscing all the enjoyable recollections of our days and hurried to the hospital. Shakthi always used to tell me a story while playing with my cheeks. "You were so tiny, pink, and your eyes were closed tightly. The Nurse showed you and told me that you were my sister. I touched your cheek slowly, you didn't move. You were sleeping so pretty and cute. I didn't have a camera. But I just took a picture with my eyes, and I still remember that moment like it happened yesterday." I get irritated whenever she plays with my cheeks, but I enjoyed her moment of happiness.

I never had the experience of seeing a new-born baby until this moment. I reached the hospital, and my sister delivered a beautiful baby girl. Shakthi was unconscious and was sleeping well because of the labour pain. I lifted the baby and started looking at her in amazement. Now I know how Shakthi must have felt when she saw me for the first time. I was telling the baby how lucky she is to have a mother like my sister. I was waiting for her to open her eyes so I could tell her, "How I met her baby." Opposite poles attract each other, while the same poles repel each other. But all of them have the same magnetic field and the same magnetic force. Even though Shakthi and I don't have anything in common, I am her magnetic field, and she is my magnetic force.

2

My Friend From Heaven, Dadoba

by Anurag Mallick

Friends. Who are called friends? Well, not the television sitcom but the friends that an individual has in real life. One we remember in times of sorrow, the shoulder one needs to borrow, the ones with which we celebrate, the ones with whom we do not hesitate. These are friends. Although there is no perfect definition for friends or the bond we share, this is what I call, friends. The bond we share, Friendship. Everyone has their first-ever friend in life. The most special one. The one you can't ever let go of. The first one you think of after doing everything. Well, enough of building the character and suspense, let me introduce to everyone reading this story, my friend, whom I call 'Dadoba'.

You might be wondering what Dadoba means? Is it a nickname? No, it isn't. Dadoba means Grandpa. Yes. My maternal Grandpa, Sri Naba Kumar Banerjee. I call him Dadoba. I met him for the first time when I came into this world. At the railway Hospital in Kharagpur. Well people who don't know about Kharagpur, Let me give you an insight into the place. It is famous for two things. The railways and the IIT. It was the World's longest railway platform for many years with 1072.5 M (3,519 ft.). It is now the third-longest.

So, when I came into this world, he was there to receive me at the hospital and was on Cloud-9. I was the first grandchild of the family. A new generation began with me. He used to call me "Dadubhai". The name I would die to listen, only from his mouth. You'll understand how it must feel when a new-born comes to the world. In general, happiness in the family had no bounds. Right from the moment I came, he treated me as his friend & not like a grandson. Well, don't most of the grandparents do that? I believe they are only meant to spread love. That's what the latter stage of life has in store for you. After all the hustle, it's time to be happy & peaceful. To enjoy family and to become a child again.

Taking me for a walk, narrating me stories, holding me in his lap, taking me for a cycle ride, taking me through the garden, singing me to sleep cuddling along. That gave me and him the most happiness. It was like he found himself in me. Those were the days when he and I lived life like there's no tomorrow. Absolutely carefree. Who knew what life had in store for us. That I would be brought far away from him to a different place. Both of us had tears in our eyes. Tears rolled down and never stopped. Doesn't that happen with every one of you when you part ways with your friends? The ones you have a soul-to-soul connection with? It does. It does. Because you know, a part of you is with them. It shall always be.

As he has been the bigger child at heart, he did not wait for me to come back to him. He came to me instead. They say, 'You only do things that you once dreamt about for people you love.' That is what he did because that is how much he loves me & that is how much, I love him back. When we met each other, it was like we had the world with us. He only knew to spread happiness. Maybe that is what he was meant for. Every time he came to meet me, he made sure he brought something that I love. Forget about me going to him that would be no less than a grand celebration. Nonetheless, it was a party.

He used to work for the Indian railways. Having a degree in English honours, I still wonder how he ended up making engines.

Coming back to us, each day was a carnival with him. You might think, what did we do to call it a carnival? I'll tell you. Gradually as I grew up, things that we did, changed. Our daily routine was first to read the newspaper (he was the one who read it and I just imitated him) and then have our signature style breakfast. Have you guys ever tried eating leftover chapatis and tea for breakfast? That is what we ate when we were together in each other's company. Spreading our legs, placing the cup of tea in between and rolling the chapathi and then dipping it in a hot cup of tea. That is by far the best thing I've eaten for breakfast. I don't think I will ever put anything on top of this, ever. Once we were done with our breakfast, we were glued to the television, watching the news. Although I couldn't understand one bit, I used to stare at the TV and imitate his expressions. He would then take me for a walk through the garden on his lap or shoulders and explained the importance of each and every plant. Then, he would leave for work.

As soon as he returned, the first thing he did was to take me for a trip on his cycle. Then come back, sit alongside me and eat fruits. Especially Litchi. The best part of the evening was when he spoke to me about his day and how it went, and I reacted to him by blabbering something in my language. He still knew I was happy. Of course, I was, as I was with him. As time passed by and I grew up, our routine changed. The breakfast remained the same, the morning and evening walk remained the same. Only our discussions would change. Our interests in things would surprisingly be similar. Isn't there a saying, "Like minds think alike?" It was like that was made for us. That is how similar we were.

As I grew up and learnt new things, he made sure I had an idea of how things worked and also knew what I wanted. There was this time where I must have been 3-4 years old. All my friends and cousins had a robot toy. This is way back in the early 2000s. When I felt left out that I didn't have one, he surprisingly brought an even better one for me. Trust me when I say this, no one in the family told him that I didn't have one or I wanted one. It was his intuition that he had brought it for me. It cost around Rs 1000/- in those days. That is how connected we were. He knew what I wanted. What I needed. He fulfilled all my wishes without even me asking. That's how he knew me. Inside out. I still have the robot with one of its hands broken. That shall always be in my cupboard. The special one.

As I grew up with time, my mindset changed, and he made sure he was always updated. He had made a habit of teaching me the names of all the fruits in English so that I would learn the language soon. That is how he was also my first teacher. I say this because there are so many things that he has taught me in life. I only cherish them. I shall always do, holding them close to my heart.

I still vividly remember whenever he came to visit me. He used to drop me to school, wait until I came back and then used to take me for a walk. I used to hold on to his little finger and walk along with him and reach a nearby bakery. One thing that I ate every day was a scoop of Vanilla ice cream.

This was my daily routine with Dadoba. Another memorable thing that I fondly remember is when he gave me a 5 rupee coin every day after I came back from school. I was so habituated to this, that once he left, I cried every evening because he went back and couldn't give me Rs 5.

Once he went back, he made sure he spoke to me every day, easily for an hour. Whenever he would speak, he began saying one thing. "Dadubhai, Kamon acho?" (Grandson, how are you?) His husky voice was to die for. Irrespective of how I fared in school, he never yelled at me. He said instead, "Shono Dadubhai, bhalo kore podashona kore, Bodo hotehobe." (Listen, Grandson, you have to study well and do well in life.) That has to be the best motivational line I would ever have to listen to when I'm down or low.

If I have to name one thing that we bonded over the most, it would be cricket. I have this mad love for the sport. From a very very young age. Although I'm not good at playing, I just love the sport. It's because he taught me everything about it. I owe it to him, completely. He was also a football fanatic. An ardent Mohanbagan FC fan. But we bonded over cricket. With how little I understood of the sport, he made sure I was perfect in it. He used to make me sit on his lap and both of us would watch cricket matches for 3-4 hours straight. He passed on his knowledge and insights to me, and I am forever grateful to him for that. There is this fond and a very dear memory I share with him. More like a promise.

Another special instance that is fresh in my mind is when it was Diwali. I was 7. The year was 2005. I asked him for a toy gun and reels (The one that kids use during Diwali). It was around 2 pm and under scorching heat, he cycled around 7-8 km only to get me that gun. There was not a single thing that I asked, and he hadn't provided. Usually, my parents always gave me one pack of reels which usually consist of about 5-6 reels. They never gave me more than that. But him being him, he brought me an entire box of reels which had around 40-50 reels. He always made sure I never fell short of anything. That is the kind of person he was.

This memory takes me back to the year 2009. The second edition of the ICC T20 World Cup was going on. We were watching a warm-up match between India & Pakistan. Suddenly during the match, I remember asking for a pair of batting gloves. He immediately said, "You need a pair of gloves, you'll get it." I was so happy. My happiness knew no bounds. One of the batsmen was just hitting boundaries. He then said, "I like players who hit the ball far and hard." From that moment even I started liking players who played that way.

Somehow for the first time, I didn't get it. Maybe he had planned giving it to me but couldn't or something else. But he didn't give me that. On the other side, I thought, "Dadoba has promised me. He will keep his promise."

Time passed by and two years down the lane, his health deteriorated and then the inevitable happened. He had left the world and settled in heaven. November 15, 2011. The day he left me alone. The worst part was that I got to know about his demise after 7 days. It's because my tests were going on. I feel he didn't even want me to lose focus from the tests and so I was unaware. You might call it foolish but that is how I think. How can he affect my studies when he motivated me and pushed me to do my best?

It's almost 9 years since he left me all alone. All I have of him are the memories that I shall hold on and live for life. I have a navy-blue round neck tee which he wore in his last days. That t-shirt fits me perfectly and I shall cherish it with me forever.

I would like to share one thing that I feel he is the reason for, and he has done. On the occasion of my birthday in 2018, a very special person gifted me a pair of batting gloves. That was the most unexpected gift I have ever received. The gloves also had a letter with it. All that was written in that letter are the same words he used to tell me. I feel he is the reason behind me getting what I wanted. How could he not fulfil my wish, even though he isn't present here physically? I shall always believe that he is the one who in the form of that special person has gifted me those gloves. That shall remain my most prized possession for life.

At the end of this beautiful fairy-tale-like story of mine, I would only like to say that your Dadubhai loves you and shall love you always. Thank you for keeping your promise. You shall always be a man of your words. Hope you're doing well up there, Old man!

Love,

Dadubhai.

3

Dear Ma

by Meghana Parasa

E verybody has a presence in their life that inspires them to be the best they can be, a role model you look up to and think – this is the person I want to be when I grow up; the most influential person that has been a part of your life. And for me, it's my mom.

The first person to teach you about love is a mother. She sacrifices her time, body, energy and sometimes even her dreams for your happiness. Where would we be without our mothers?

My mom's name is Dr. P. Madhavi. She is an ENT surgeon working at her clinic. My mom has been a single parent and the sole provider for two kids (me and my little brother) since my dad passed away in a horrible accident in 2005. We were at the tender ages of 6 and 2 years respectively and did not understand the gravity of the situation. She worked to her bones to support us and provide for all our dreams.

These days, I'm always out with friends, studying, working, or just hanging out in my room watching the newest episode of any show on Netflix. As I grow older, I seem to have forgotten about the people who got me to where I am, and I've especially forgotten about the one person who pushed me to make me into the person I've become, my mother.

So, I am writing this open letter to my mother in a small effort to show how grateful I am for the life she has provided for me.

To the most beautiful person in the world,

Dear Ma,

Let me start by saying thank you. Thank you for all the love and support. Although it might seem like empty words after everything you have ever done for me, I love you ma. Even though I do not say it enough, I try my best to show it through actions. I know you have always been frustrated about my inability to express myself, but you should know, you are the greatest of them all. I can never love anyone as much as I love you.

Everything I am now, I owe it to you. Everything from my love for math to my work ethic traces back to you. I am thankful every day that I get to call you my mom.

Life is overwhelming and chaotic, but you always knew what matters the most in your life, and for you, it's your family.

One of my earliest memories of you was not letting you leave for work. I sulked, pouted, cried, and made a huge fuss every morning even though I knew you were going to come back soon. Looking back, I realize how hard it must have been for you to leave your little girl at home. You worked yourself into exhaustion every day just so you could afford to continue to support your children. And when you came back you always made sure to spend time with us, it did not matter that you were standing in the operation theatre all day or that you were treating sick people. We always came first.

You have always inspired and motivated me to be the best version of myself. I owe all my success to the lessons you have taught me.

I remember this one time; I was trying to finish an assignment. I did the usual, copy information from Wikipedia, print some pictures, slap them together and voila! It's done. You took one look at my assignment and were shocked. It is funny when I think back and remember the horrified expression on your face. You showed me how to organize the information and make it presentable. I did not understand what the big deal was at first. But when the grades were out, I was surprised to see that I scored an A+. I learned one of the greatest life lessons that day, how we present ourselves and our work matters a great deal.

One of my favourite memories we share is you teaching me math in seventh grade. I had always been an average student and my grades were starting to slip. You took some time off from your work just so you can help me with my math. That term I scored a 100 per cent for the first time in my life. It made me realize if I work for it, no matter what the goal, I can achieve it. It was then that I started to love math and analytical problems. I have topped math ever since.

Thank you for never giving up on me Ma, for believing I can do better even when I did not believe so myself.

I am sure you and I both agree that my teenage years were a mess. I put you through a lot of trouble. But you had always been understanding and patient with all my tantrums. You helped me find a way out of all the mess. Your love and strength have always pulled me out of any difficult situation I have been in. For every mistake I have committed, you supported me and encouraged me to do the right thing. You taught me that everybody commits mistakes, but what matters is the way you handle it.

Love. You showed me how unconditional your love is. Through thick and thin your love for me has never wavered. When I was going through a phase of depression and felt nothing in life made sense, I asked you how you were able to do it. Life has not been kind to you. You lost your mother at a young age and your husband 10 years later. You have been through hell. And yet you stand strong in the face of adversity. You told me:

"My strength comes from my love for you kids. I can fight anything that life throws at me if it means my kids are happy and fulfilled."

Your answer changed the whole perspective of my life. I realized how valuable every second of life is and how you make my life worth living. Thank you for making sure that I knew I was loved every second of my life and letting me know it's okay to make mistakes and that it's okay to cry.

For every difficulty thrown your way, you have faced them without giving up. Thank you for teaching me to face my problems instead of quitting. It is a mantra I try to live by every day- I have to face the situation no matter how scary, and that I might as well do the best I can.

I admire your faith in God. After all that you have been put through, you pray daily. You have always prayed for us and I guess those prayers will protect me throughout my life. Without a single doubt, you are the most resilient and faithful person ever. I wish you nothing but happiness in your future.

You deserve it more than anybody in this world.

You showed me there is more to life than just studies and jobs. You nurtured the creativity in me. You drove me to music classes, tennis classes and art classes. You made sure I spent my time and energy efficiently. Today I can appreciate the beauty in the little things surrounding us.

You are not just a role model in life but also my professional career. You are one of the best doctors in the state. I see how grateful patients are when all their ailments are heard. You showed me that being a doctor is not just about the medication and surgeries. It is understanding the patient's problem and making the decision that is best for them. You have treated your patients like they are your third child. When I see how much you have accomplished, it makes me proud to call you my mother.

Remember the day dad died? It was a normal evening almost at the end of summer. I had finished all my homework for the day and was waiting for you and daddy to come home. Who knew one call could change a family's life forever? It was devastating. I did not understand much of anything happening around me. I was still expecting dad to walk in through the door any minute, with maybe a broken arm or leg. But he never came.

You never let your kids see you crying and suffering after that day because you knew we were already vulnerable. And seeing you like that only made us sadder and lonelier. You never complained once that life was unfair. You always battled every challenge you faced. You never made us feel like we were inadequate or a burden. Thank you for going out of your way to make my life so valuable and priceless.

Even though we do not remember much of our dad, you

always made sure he was alive in our memories. You made sure that we remembered him as the perfect man in the whole wide world.

You are the strongest person I know mama. Even after dad passed away you fought hard in a male-dominated society and became successful. You taught me to be independent and always work hard for what you want. You never once strayed from your beliefs even when it was extremely hard. As a kid, I was naïve and had no idea how hard it is for a single mother to survive in a judgmental and conservative society like ours. As I grew aware of the problems you face every day that I felt guilty for not being able to be of much help. I promise you, mama, that I will make you proud. I will never let you go through any difficulty alone ever again.

You have not just given me the gift of life, but also the greatest present I have ever cherished- a little brother. Thanks to Nitin, I have always been entertained. I get to do all sorts of things from fighting with him to dishing on people we do not like. I love that I have a partner in crime. I can share just about anything with him. Today when all three of us are spending time doing useless things like watching tv, eating together or playing cards, I live in my perfect little world. Also, I will beat you both at rummy someday, this isn't over yet! I love our endless chats, our jokes and wish to create as many memories as possible.

I should let you know Ma, it never mattered to us that we were being raised by a single parent. You never let us feel inadequate in any aspect of life. You always made sure to attend every one of my activities and cheered me on. Thanks to you I am confident to face the world.

Just when I thought our lives are set for smooth sailing, you were diagnosed with breast cancer. Even if it may not seem like it, the news has hit me harder than ever. For a couple of days, it felt like the universe is punishing me for reasons unknown to me. But your strength and optimism, even though it was you must go through so much trauma again, motivated me to look at the positives of this situation. This is a chance for me to prove myself a worthy daughter and repay a part of everything you have done for me so far. Bear with me as I strive to be a better version of myself every day so I can take care of you. I hope I can make your recovery as comfortable as possible.

Lastly, I want to tell you I am sorry. I am sorry for all the times I fought with you and let you down. I am sorry for the times I chose other people and things over you. Sometimes I tend to lose sight of the things that are most important to me. You truly mean so much to me Mumma and I do not tell you enough. I will try to be a better person, who pays attention to you. I hope that by the time I am older you can someday forgive me for acting like this.

You are not just a mother to me but also my father, grandmother, friend, teacher, and my saviour. You are my superhero. Thank you for trusting me and letting me be myself, for loving me just the way I am, flaws and all. I hope to live up to your standards as a mother, a teacher, a doctor, a wife and most importantly as a human. It would be my greatest achievement in life is the day I hear the words "You have become your mom." I have always loved you and will continue to love you forever. I hope you remember that no matter where life takes us, you are the best mom a daughter could ever ask for.

"The best feeling in the world is knowing I am a little piece of you – Clearissa Lynn Castaneda."

Your daughter for 22 years

Parasa Meghana (Raji)

4

The Mango Tree, Shopping Lists, And Nine-Volt Batteries

by Laasya Pemmaraju

In memory of my beloved grandfather

There's an arrangement to the existence of a few; history assumes that it is for the best to wear them down soon enough. Nothing is too puzzling to those who try to decipher how mundane their lives were and will ever be. Mundane enough to delight those who wish the same, with the simplicity, the wisdom and the everlasting impact of a still demise. The world aligns to make them exist and takes them away when it feels it is enough. For the cynical half of us, it seems appropriate for perception to narrate their stories. Perception is an old friend that never fails those who believe in it. For, there is no way it can manipulate what is right, yet so fickle it is, to not let one see for what it exactly is. No one ever questions how they perceive; it is always what they see.

At the end of every city dwells the suburban life that seems to have the answer to the universe through its modesty. Sometimes Al wondered if the mango tree in the courtyard had seen the better part of her childhood. The mango tree for one knew that she was Al and not Alia anymore. But if the mango tree's denied voyeurism through its branches, leaves and the tinted glass, enough to narrate Al and her grandfather, then how about the shopping lists?

It was a breezy spring afternoon. A season after, on a rather chilly morning, Al's grandfather would pass away. The irony at the beginning of this apposition was not lost on Al. Al assigned Alia at birth, never assumed to suffer the consequences of a surprisingly monotonous upbringing for such a family of flair. She often rebelled against her causes even. There was a sense of comfort she found in defiance; especially for causes that did not entail her. This struck the perfect balance between resistance and denial.

There she was, standing in the hallway, trying so hard to read the room beyond the door. All to unravel the mystery of her mother's thoughts. An unexplainable haze enveloped everything apart from their eyes. Al, just dramatizing the moment while waiting for it to end was as real as her thoughts could fool her. Behind the haze was a wound that was just about to form, holding up for her mother to reject her idea, which shall persist as a memory. To her surprise, Al for the first time in years was given errands to run, under the condition that someone accompanies her. The truth is, Al had gone to a shrink for three years, the one that prescribed her pills and diagnosed to be 'self-destructive with the inclination to blow up everyone around', on multiple accounts. But, how would she tell her mother that she knew better than the man in a white coat? Al's grandfather joined to go shopping with her that afternoon.

Al's grandfather was a man of discipline and cultural nuance. He was someone that she did not seem to mind living under the same roof with. She often found herself thinking, "What can archaic understanding and compromises bring to the table in the age of resistance and intolerance?". Al's brother, however, revelled in the masculinity that his grandfather offered, a connection solely established on a patriarchal warmth that did not play harmful. Al's brother Jai was ten years old when he had discovered that Al did not fit into his understanding of who a female is, "Whoa! What are you doing? Are you not a girl?", he would often exclaim. It was not too late before he had understood that Al had secrets that would overwhelm him, loads of them, and that it was best to leave her to them. Not that he had the mettle to settle on hers without disclosing his, but his secrets do not weigh much in comparison.

Al's grandfather, on the other hand, would often seem to question more than what she appeared to make known. Under normal circumstances, despite being withdrawn, Al would try with her grandfather a touch of warmth in their interactions. Something about physical fragility accompanying years meant more feebleness than just as much to Al. Despite being in touch with her self-assured masculinity, her grandfather's imposition did more than merely shake Al's conception of her identity. Growing up, she subconsciously despised traditional masculinity; it invalidated her existence, adding more reason to her comprehension of her grandfather. Something about this man did not exude vulnerability even at a fragile age to her and the very presence of conserved conscience entertained distress at her expense. Everything her grandfather did to her was as though he was flaunting his authority over her, and for his sternness, he did not seem to disagree either. He did in some ways want to hold his dear withering life from slipping away into loathing taciturnity.

Her hesitance certainly did not prove useful to her desire to enjoy fresh spring draft, waltzing on her toes, through the fleeting bakery wind, and neither did she graze along the trunk of the beloved mango tree. To Al, her grandfather does not see the struggle behind her skittish knees hitting the ground before she could appeal in return for her displayed rationality, prudence and obedience. What if the dreaded psychiatrist was right and she was to blow up after all? Her docility clouded overbearing, it appeared to have cleared her chaos after all; anything was better than insufferable chastising at her expense.

Escaping what home was to Al, resulted in her never turning down a chance to run along for errands. For the next couple of times that grandfather had accompanied Al, he would often seem relaxed, and to her surprise, she found his company rather restful. As the trail ends and they reach the shop, Al would stumble across the tiny counter fronting an even tinier popup shed, which was far from being a store. By now, she had successfully recited all the things in order, while the shopkeeper, perched on a broken stool, reached out with his meek arms to grab the first thing on the list from the shelves. The shelves were stacked way up and beyond their peripheral.

After for what seemed like an eternity in the purgatory for those who despised silence, Al's grandfather steadied his eyes, while his veiny, trembling fingers had reached his pocket to draw out a shopping list. He turned to Al and giggled "You will not hear the end of it otherwise, eh?". Al quickly acknowledged his remark, realising that she did forget Jai's request, and so squealed "...And a set of Nine-Volt batteries!" at the shopkeeper. The shopkeeper was now visibly side eyeing her for making him climb up on his stool again. She followed a smile at her grandfather in embarrassment now that her wall of aloofness had blown up.

She now realised that she would not have heard the end of Jai cribbing. He would say that without those batteries, the headlights on his remote-control truck he had gotten for Diwali, "are as dull as Al before drinking her first coffee in the morning". Her grandfather retreated the shopping list back into his pocket without even glancing at it. She was quick enough to recognise his act of solidarity and contemplated on it on their way back home.

"Does he trust me enough after all? Does this mean he would believe me when I tell him that my counsellor did me no good?"

Al sunk into her pillow before she even knew.

Over the next couple of times, Al would let go of all her fears the moment she grazed her hand along the trunk of the mango tree in her courtyard, which now became a ritual; then, was once an inhibition. A ritual convincing her transcending into a safe space, an idea that had failed her before.

Al and grandfather got along pretty well now. They would chat about their day, starting from how Miriam at school wore the worst pair of pants Al had ever seen, to how Jai and his obsession with his Nine-Volt batteries were robbing mom of her savings. A few minutes later, how Al's grandmother was recovering from a self-yapping syndrome: a name Al and grandfather gave to grandmother's sleeping talking, and finally, to how Al's shrink keeps prescribing her these sweet pills. Al has always been quick to accuse them of being "nothing but sugar pills that are placebic". She was smart enough to start appreciating the outlet that venting out to her grandfather had given her. Spring was kind to Al, a season that seemed to empathise with all her repressed emotions, trauma, agony; a gift and opportunity that was never seized early on.

The universal truth is that Spring has to make way. As summer approaches, the mango tree in the courtyard budded with life, Al would spend most of her time looking out the window locked up in her room. On a hot afternoon, as she approached the kitchen, a loud thump against the floor in the foyer echoed. Al still in shock from the sight collapsed on the floor next to her grandfather, the next thing Al remembered was the horrifying sight of endless hospital doors flinging across a boundless bright tunnel. A tunnel that never saw its end for its good; overloading her senses. Al would spend the next couple of hours, awake and distraught through the night. The morning was unusually chilly indeed. An announcement later was this bizarre feeling of harmony. Al did not like that she was thoughtless, an emptiness that for once was not the void.

A monologue. "Void would deprive the meaning of life and the meaning of all the moments in my life I did not cherish… A void would disgrace an existence, an existence that cannot be celebrated anymore. A life that existed before I breathed, and the feeling of altruism calling my thoughts out… To have chosen suffering over peace; and if that meant that I had to suffer, was that what he wanted for me?".

Thoughts racing were merely thoughts anymore, but why would they not translate into tears? To Al, sobbing was a masquerading epiphany that she craved for that minute.

Her mother sauntered across, and slipped Al a box, who was now bracing herself on a staircase; against life, death, and every philosophical pondering that Santa Muerte had fed her brain.

A wooden box, whose deliberate countenance even went out of its way for an endeavour in epitomizing its contents. How baffling it was, to see the contrast in value. The chiselled pattern along the hinges made the box gorily enough, resemble a casket. What would Al guard it with? Would an ambiguous serpent lock suffice? Or maybe a vault that did not test her worth? These were more than just words beyond the grave. Her fingers felt at all the ridges on the box. She knew that it was time for her to open the box.

There was nothing left. Nothing more than her and the moment. Al looked infinite, fantastical even; better than she ever knew of herself. For her epiphany had finally occurred. Tears accompanied her pale look of omniscience and the gait that is of a fallen geisha. By now, fragility visibly sept through her eyes and for another conscience that did not know any better; it was what would have been a steady race between her breath and the clock. It was her and a legacy of these shopping lists against the world.

5

Ima

by Rosalind Princess Reshma

I like to think I am not an emotional person. In situations where others get angry or upset, I tend to stay calm and keep asking questions until I get my point across. I often initiate arguments but never participate in them. I let the emotionally weak opponents have a one-sided argument until they start contradicting themselves. The only tears I remember shedding recently are the ones that escaped my eyes after the first bite of a very spicy chicken wing.

But today, I'm crying. All I want to do is curl up on the floor and cry till there are no tears left in my eyes. And then scream till my throat begins to drown my voice.

I have often wondered why poets and romantics associate the heart with love.

"You can't love with your heart." I used to tell people. "It's the brain that does all the thinking, including love. Technically you love with your brain."

I liked killing beauty with the sharp sword of logic.

But now, I understand that the poets were always right. When I heard the news, I felt like an invisible hand had ripped out my heart from my ribcage and left a bitter heart-shaped pain in the emptiness.

"Hey, do you remember that old lady who used to deliver milk when we were children?" the Facebook message read. "She passed away last night."

Of course, I remembered her. All of us did.

She was known as Ima- mother in Manipuri. Ima's arrival was always right before the mellow Sun disappeared behind the blue chain of hills at the horizon. It was an unusual time to deliver milk, but my mother was happy with it because it meant fresh milk for her evening tea. For me, it meant the unfair and unceremonious end to my outdoor playtime. To avoid protests, my mother came up with a clever plan.

"I can see that you are a big girl now," she told me one fine day.

Now, those are the magical words every child wants to hear.

"And I thought I could trust you with big responsibilities." she continued as I suppressed a grin behind my tightly shut lips.

"What is it? I tried not to sound too excited. What if she changed her mind?

"If you can stand outside every evening and collect the milk, it would be a great help," she said. "The other day, I was too tired to wait so I kept the container out. By the time I came to collect the milk, it was spilt."

"But our Rexy doesn't do that." I was afraid she might ask me to abandon my little ginger cat.

"Of course, he doesn't. Must be some other cat."

"Or a bird." I was not willing to accept that cats can be

vicious creatures.

"Yes. It could be a bird," she said. "So, would you take up the responsibility of collecting the milk?"

I was in a dilemma. This responsibility would mean I cannot spend my evenings with the other children, looking for golden tortoise beetles in the tall grass. But then some sacrifices had to be made.

"I will, mother," I assured her.

The next day, I had great plans of carrying out my first responsibility. Unfortunately, I had to encounter Ima with a scraped knee and a muddy face. She did not say anything. She quietly filled the steel canister and the Rexy's little bowl. She studied my teary face and motioned me to wipe away my tears. She didn't speak my language. I did not understand hers. But that didn't stop her from doing her part in making a little child smile. She held my hand and led me across the path and pointed at the bushes. Confused, I looked at the bush and then at her. It must have been very obvious because she laughed and muttered something that could have only meant, 'Silly child, look carefully!' She took my hand once again and made me touch a leaf and to my surprise, the leaf shrunk as if it was hiding from me. As if it was protecting a secret from my vicious touch. The painful knee was immediately forgotten as I began to look for that strange leaf all over the place.

That night I learned that it was fondly called 'touch-me-not'. That out there in the vast world there was a plant exactly like me, shying away from the slightest touch.

Soon, Ima's arrival became something I looked forward to. She would show me something new every day. A pretty flower. Grass that holds sweet sap. Leaves like elephants' ears that held dewdrops and remnants of rain like sparkling diamonds. Caterpillars and strange bugs. Millipedes that rolled into a ball at a hint of danger. Leeches that waited for careless children to step into the wet mud. Butterflies larger than my palms. Each day she would open my eyes to a new wonder of nature, and I loved her for that.

It was a strange friendship between a woman who had seen everything life could throw at her and a child who was yet to be disillusioned by the world. A relationship without words. A relationship that began and thrived on the patch of grass that was greener than any other, with glimmers of other colours. It would be years before I read Wordsworth's famous, 'Nature never did betray the heart that loved her'. Ima had already taught me in her simple gestures that nature would never fail to make me happy.

Within a few months, she became one of the important people in my life and I like to believe I was important to her too. I had a reason to believe it. On my ninth birthday, she gifted me a fountain pen. She said she couldn't stay for the cake cutting as she had to go to other houses to deliver milk. So, I gave her some chocolates and she placed her hand on my head and wished for a long and prosperous life for me. And then she pulled out a small newspaper-wrapped gift and pressed it against my palms. I thanked her with a hug. Later that night, my father told me that the pen was expensive, and that Ima must have saved up her hard-earned money to buy it for me. I felt guilty about it but I also felt special.

I lost it eventually. I don't remember how. I had it till my first board exam in tenth grade. I wasn't planning on using it but wanted it around as a good luck charm. I don't remember losing it or looking for it. It became one of the things whose absence you get accustomed to overtime and try to put your finger on that exact moment it ceased existing in your life.

Like hope. Like a lot of things, you believe in till you behold reality.

I feel a fresh wave of grief as I remember the pen. That could have been a piece of her love I could have held on to had I not lost it.

The shrill noise of my ringtone shakes me out of my memories. Reluctantly, I decided to attend the call.

"You won't believe this!" I hear a familiar voice.

Mini and I have been friends since kindergarten, and we have somehow managed to remain so all these years. Distance and time did stretch the thread that connects us, but they never managed to snap it. We don't talk often but we make sure we drop a text message regularly. She wouldn't call me if it weren't important.

"Believe what?" I ask.

"I went to Ima's house. To offer condolences."

"You did? What time is it anyway?"

"It's 6 PM! Whatever, so..."

"Wait, so I've been crying this whole time? I got the news about Ima's...I mean I got the news in the morning. I didn't realize I had spent that kind of time grieving."

"I get it. Even I cried a lot. It was difficult to explain to my husband why I am crying so much over a milkmaid...or milk lady...or whatever we could call her... So, I get it. I knew you'd be upset. All of us are."

"So, you met her family?"

Oh yes, that's what I was going to tell you. You won't believe this. Remember, when we were little, Ima would tell us that she has a granddaughter our age? That granddaughter had flown in from London. I was talking to her..."

"Wow! It's a good thing. At least her grandchildren are doing better."

"Er...that's what I was thinking till she told me that they were always doing 'better'. Turns out they have been landlords for generations. They have always owned land and have always had a steady income from agriculture and of course, their cows. The house they live in was built years ago by Ima's husband. I was shocked when I saw that palatial building."

"What?"

"Yes! They are rich! Ima was rich. Can you believe that? And here I was feeling guilty because she gifted me a fancy pencil box on one of my birthdays!"

"Wait, she gifted you a pencil box? She gave me a fountain pen once."

Mini laughs.

"I'm not surprised," she says. "All the children who grew up there have gotten something from her. And I'm not talking about fancy pens and pencil boxes. I'm talking about the love for nature she taught us all. She showed me how to grow moss. Before I met her, I used to think mosses were gross. But the day she coerced me into removing my sneakers and feeling their velvety softness on my bare feet, I fell in love with them. Even now I have a moss garden on my balcony, and I think about her when my tired feet touch them every evening."

"She was one of a kind, wasn't she?" Now, I'm smiling through my tears.

"Yeah. And she was going around delivering milk by herself even though she could have easily hired someone to do it. I got to know she was doing it till a day before she passed. And she was eighty-five! Can you imagine? I'm thirty and I don't want to get up to put my teacup in the sink."

"Tell me all about it!"

"And her granddaughter was telling me that she loved doing it not just because she loved her independence but also because she got to meet children. She loved spending time with us… Which brings me back to the reason I called...wait, I'm sending you a photo. Check!"

I open the image and I am stupefied. I see a handmade 'get well soon' card. With imperfect flowers drawn with crayons and scribbles that barely look like words.

I don't remember exactly when but once, we heard that Ima was down with viral fever and that there would be no milk for a week. While the adults were upset about the chalky taste of dairy whitener in their tea, their children decided to make a card for the woman who meant so much to them. There were around nine of us and each one of us got to draw or write something. I drew a sunflower. I had run out of yellow crayons, so I used orange. We didn't know how to give her, so we waited. A week later, when she came with her milk canisters and bright smile, we ran up to her and gave her the card. She took a look at it and placed it carefully inside her tote.

I look at the orange sunflower on my screen and realize how stupid I must have been to think that sunflower could be anything but yellow.

"She kept it." Mini's voice comes through.

"I can see that", I said, unable to take away my eyes from the picture.

"She remembered us all till the very end." Mini is about to cry. "She remembered us all...our names and what we liked."

"Guess what, you take your time. We can talk later."

"Thank you for not making this awkward. I don't want to cry while I'm talking… Bye then."

As she hangs up, I realize that Mini was right. It doesn't matter if I lost that pen. I still have a more precious gift that Ima gave me. Her memories will live on as long as I breathe. In the dew on my lawn, in the scent of the first rain, in the eucalyptus tree at my bedroom window, in the song of the skylarks and in every little thing that makes this world beautiful. And if I want I can make her memories live a little longer.

I look at the clock as the doorbell rings. I open the door and let in my son who runs into the kitchen and opens the fridge with his muddy hands.

"What did I tell you?" I tell him in the sternest tone I can muster.

"I wasn't touching the food. I'm thirsty."

"But what did I tell you?"

"Okay," he says, placing the water bottle on the counter. "I'll take a shower first."

"You better wash off all that sand from your hair, a young man and the clothes go into the laundry bag. I don't want sand on my bed."

He doesn't answer. I know he's going to leave his clothes on the bed.

Tomorrow, I'll take him to the garden and show him butterflies and ladybirds. I'll show him dew on a blade of grass. If we're lucky, we might find a touch-me-not. And then I will tell him about my childhood home, Manipur. The land of jewels where one can find bugs the colour of gold. And I will tell him about Ima.

6

The Baldpate Man

by Raga Lahari

As usual, it is a busy day thinking. How tough is the job of a writer? I muttered pitying myself. There are always stacks of novels staring at me with the same old desperate glare for salvation. The clock promptly ticked five in the evening and a feathery lightness came over me. It was that time for me to walk down to the stall and have my rejuvenating cup of coffee. I just have to say "Anna" and he'll bring my cup in a blink of an eye. Today was no different.

When I stood at the stall enjoying each sip, I saw a head from behind that felt familiar. He was a thin old man in a blue shirt with a bald head, standing by his silver bicycle parked at a distance. I felt a tsunami of joyfulness inside of me. My heartbeat was more than usual. My excitement knew no bounds. I walked quickly to him and laid my left hand on his left shoulder. His turning back was one beautiful slow motion full of suspense. In my mind, I had already framed sentences and repeated them over and over again. *There he is. Alas! After fifteen years!* I thought. Meanwhile, my excitement and joy vanished into thin air the moment he looked in my eye and inquired "Yes?". I bent my head down and replied, "Sorry. I was mistaken. I thought you were someone known to me". I felt a sudden thud in the atmosphere. I left six rupees on Anna's counter and walked back silently. I sat on my chair with an intense sigh, closed my eyes and slid into thoughts. *C'mon, do it. Now!* was the loudest thought I heard at the moment. I immediately picked my pen, wrote swiftly on a white paper "Dear Postman Uncle" and paused. A wide smile clung to my face. My mind began reminiscing about the past and I kept talking to myself.

I didn't know his name. I never asked him either. I was twelve and he was thirty-six when I first saw him. He was a jolly postman sharply aiming letters that landed straight into the basket hanging to the gate. A perfect long curve is what I can imagine if he launches a letter. Postman Uncle was of average height, thin in structure, almost baldpate, with healthy, glowing eyes, always pedalling on his silver bicycle in the lanes of my colony. He smiled like it was his second nature.

His presence itself was a warm sight for everyone in the neighbourhood. His energy escalated as he aged. 4:30 p.m. was the time I could watch him sing, swing, and deliver all the letters with a cheerful face. One day, he stopped by and asked me, "Which class Beta?" in a fruity tone that was deep, strong, and incomparable. I responded, "Sixth Uncle." I know today that our journey began right then and right there.

On the very next day, at 4:30 p.m. again, I saw him launching letters while he sang the then-latest hit melody. I might have intruded into his sweet world, but I stopped his cycle anyway and asked curiously, "Uncle, don't you want to open all the letters you have? Are you not curious to read them all?" He guffawed at once while pulling my cheeks. "I am only interested in letters that come for me, Beta," came his reply. Ah! Such lies, my brain thought while my eyes rolled from northeast to northwest. He was up to date with all the life stories of my neighbours. On the other day, when Nadhiya Aunty forgot her grandson's birthday who lives in the US, it was Postman Uncle who came to her rescue.

Not only that! When Amshu Uncle was trudging up the stairs, "Congratulations sir!" he wished with a broad smile and went away biking. We learned later that he got promoted in the office. No wonder he already knew how I cheated in the Math test the other day, I thought with a little fear in my heart. Usually, he gets money when he brings in good news, but I didn't know why Tulipa Aunty gave him money when she heard that her mother-in-law passed away.

Although he was the king of information around there, he was still trusted by everyone including me, maybe because he never disclosed how I cheated in school or stole a bar of chocolate from Kapil Grandpa's shop. He was not just the newsreader but also the news keeper of the colony. My grandmother used to offer him a glass full of chilled buttermilk or water whenever he looked weary. When I asked him why he had no holidays, he only said, "Delivering letters in time was crucial, Beta." and kept cycling until he became thinner. His hundred-dollar smile along with an added 'Namasthe Beta' became my favourite in no time. Eventually, we became friends and then best friends.

He taught me how to write letters. "Today, I am writing one for you," I murmured while leaning back into the backrest of my chair. We shared ice cream together, cycled together, and even played 'Hide and Seek' together. One day, I finished my homework early, gulped my evening snack quickly and kept kicking my heels at the portico for Postman Uncle to show up. That day, I decided to ask what his name was. Is it Ramu? or Zayed? Or are you David? I thought, strolling on the walkway. It was 4:30p.m. and there was no sign of him. 6:30p.m. 9:30a.m. 4:30p.m again and still no news.

I am twenty-seven years old now and my heart still expects his presence. The colony chatter was that he got transferred to another location that nobody knew. In two more months, we shifted as well. Will any lover search and wait for their love to return as I did for you, Postman Uncle? flashed in my head. Suddenly, my heart felt heavy, and my mind felt blank. I looked at the white paper, readout, "Dear Postman Uncle" and continued to jot down as some more words passed my brain.

"......I don't want to know your name because I'll still call you 'Postman Uncle' anyway. I don't want to know your address because you still stay in my memories anyway. I want you to know that I still remember you and will always do. I don't know if you were my friend, or my teacher, or just a postman but I want you to know that I cherish and value our bond. Just one more ice cream and a short cycle ride are all that I wish for. There is a lot for you to get updated.

Lots of Love
Hari

I threw the pen aside and knocked my head to the tabletop. Years of woe set me into weeping until I experienced fatigue. Slowly, I began to feel drowsy, and sleep came upon me as a blessing. I woke up the next day with an unburdened chest. Mental calmness took a seat inside me. Suddenly I felt a glow on my face when an idea struck my mind. PUBLISH! the thought resonated. I picked my pen again, put my thoughts down until it turned into a beautiful story that gave great relief to my soul. "Hey, Readers! Remember your postman? Hey Postman! Look, you have readers!" I blabbered in high spirits. Impatiently, I submitted my write-up at the publishing house and waited every day for news about its selection while working on other write-ups. In three more days, I was informed that my story got selected and to my surprise, published as well! What can I say? I was overwhelmed with an unwelcome pride. I couldn't wait any longer to receive a copy and to experience the feeling of reading one's own published work.

After a week on a busy Monday evening, yes…as usually I was thinking. I was waiting for the clock to tick five so that I could have my coffee from Anna's stall. It was only 4:30 yet, so I continued with my work. Meanwhile, the doorbell rang and a continuous, yet sweet voice was heard faintly. I put the pen aside, got up to open the door. The voice became clearer and intelligible with every step that I took while nearing the door. "Post sir. Post." went on ceaselessly from the other end. I left the door ajar and stood behind it. Of course, it was a fond fruity voice. My excitement hiked to a limit that I broke out sobbing with joy. He opened the door widely and stood straight obstructing the bright path of the sunlight beam. There he was! Alas! After fifteen years! The thin old baldpate man standing in front of me holding a letter, a book and two cups of ice cream. I could see his silver cycle parked by the gate that brought back numerous memories. I looked at his evergreen smiling face, hugged and asked: "How?" "I am interested in reading letters that come for me, Beta." came his reply. There was a moment of silence and then we burst out laughing. I opened the seal of the letter hurriedly and indecently. The publisher wrote to me that he really liked the story and that he knew who the Postman Uncle in the story was. He also sent me the free author's copy. I looked at the book in his hands and the title was clearly visible through the gaps between his fingers. It shone boldly as 'The Loved One'

7

Love To The Heaven (From The Heaven)

by Madhurya Kommuri

Is it possible to miss someone whom you have no moments or memories with?

Hello family,

Glad to meet you all on this tragically beautiful day, for a painfully good reason.

Alright alright, I get your looks. What would I talk about this person, I didn't even see him? Right?

Does it matter?

A little tantrum, a puppy look, and the youngest one has it.

Come on, am I not the youngest of my generation? Shouldn't I use that excuse to get what I want?

(Family smiles)

There you go... See, I am not that bad.

Almost every one of you here lived with him at some point of the time or the other or at least spent some days. You experienced his love, care; felt his affection. I had none of it.

(poor me)

But I am no less than you in this matter. True you had memories, and moments; and all I have are just stories heard. But they mean something to me, actually a lot because I feel somehow grandpa has shown meaning to many things in life he became the definition of love for me. Little pieces of his stories taught how to hold my pieces together. Listening to him I don't know when I started to make him my role model, to look for him in every person. He was just amazing as a person, a husband, a father, grandfather. I know you all agree. Isn't his 25th death anniversary memorial service a good time to remind all those good old days and pay him a respectful homage?

"Love is patient, Love is kind,
It does not envy,
It does not boast, it is not proud."
Corinthians chapter 13 verse 4

I thank everyone other than blood relatives here and I am sure that we all agree that we have such amazing friends who are like family just because of grandpa. These people helping and supporting us today are proof of his kind nature. I heard a stray dog became grandpa's security guard and used to follow him to places he went for conveying God's word to people in remote places. That is how his kindness brought all living beings close and made even animals trust him. It is said that there arose some problems with our church members due to the regional difference of grandpa and it is very awful to know that believers sent local thugs to the home to threaten the family. But he showed patience by tolerating it all and did not even file a complaint against them. How much patience does one need to do it? Sure, a lot.

This question is for you all. How many of you knew that grandpa joined the army as a wireless technician against his parents wish? He ran away. Yes yes, some of you knew and I saw some surprised faces. You all know that he had to quit the job when his 2nd youngest baby girl, unfortunately, passed away. She couldn't stay without him and it caused her illness. Yeah, he left the job he got into with a lot of passion, all for the love of his family, yet he never complained and blamed nor boasted about the sacrifice he made for your well-being. Because that was his love for his family.

He was an amazing person to family, friends, neighbours, and animals too.

"Love is not rude, it is not selfish,
It is not easily angered,
It keeps no record of wrongs."
Corinthians chapter 13 verse 5

This incident makes me laugh until my belly hurts. Once when there were strands of hair in the food, he put the rice in granny's saree pallu and tied it up to her head. (Crowd's loud laughs)

And this is the only incident that made me a little bit mad at grandpa. But it was just for that moment. There might be many such incidents where he and granny had arguments, but they overcame it all. He might have been mad at her for many such things, but he didn't let those reasons overpower his love. He never held on to that anger.

Momma told me he died at the age of 70 and granny at 77 years. And she also told me that grandpa always prayed for granny's long-life but never asked for himself. Wasn't that so lovely? (#husbandgoals).

He surely was a selfless, forgiving husband.

"It does not delight in wrongdoing but rejoices with the truth."
Corinthians chapter 13 verse 6

Sure, grandpa was a man who believed in decent living with morals, being good, responsible. Discipline was very important to him. Why wouldn't it be, after all, he worked in the army.

If you don't correct your children, you don't love them. If you love them, you will be quick to discipline them.
Proverbs chapter 13 verse 24

When our elder uncle Jacob John came home late after watching the movie, grandpa told his elder daughter-in-law not to let her husband inside. He didn't want his son to be leaving his newlywed wife and have fun outside. That would be quite irresponsible.

Another incident, when the youngest two children, Aunt Shoba and my mom Flora didn't want to go to school the day after some function at home because they wanted to play with the relatives, they very smartly left for school but returned halfway giving some lame excuse. (Looking at both of them) Do you remember what happened next? (sarcastic smile) " Dad made us kneel in veranda" (overlapping voices with a painful laugh)

He wasn't hesitant to teach his son to walk on the correct path. Grandpa strongly believed in the above verse.

You people might get irritated at his strict ways but would not deny that he was the best guide you could have.

"It always protects, always trusts,
It always hopes, always perseveres."
Corinthians chapter 13 verse 7

Mumma always tells me how grandpa used to take care of you all. He would hold you in his lap when one of you is sick, how he used to put your head in his lap and clean your eyes with a wet towel when you catch some eye infection. Though you were many and grandpa was not rich to afford luxuries, how he used to wet all the curtains and tie a wet cloth around mud pot to protect you all from heat.

How big dreams he had for all of you yet left you upon your own decisions trusting your choices. He wanted Mumma to do medicine in CMC (Christian Medical College, Vellore) which didn't happen, unfortunately, but he still hoped for all good and yes good came along as she could get a secured job at the very young age of 20 years. He lost few of his children, had to quit the army job to take care of you, sometimes struggled to provide for you all yet he never gave up on his faith, he tried to spread God's word with whatever he had; he never gave up on you all, made sure you all got a good education.

He is the best father I ever knew about.

Blessed are you, the elder half of us. You got to enjoy it

with grandpa. You had so much fun with him. And we the younger half missed all of it. For you, he was a person. But for us he is just an image created in our minds from the stories we heard from you all.

I seriously envy you. But it is also good to be the youngest because after all other siblings leave, we get to spend with them the most in their last days, just like mom did with grandpa. And maybe that's why mom got to know him like no other of her siblings got to. And maybe that's how I am standing in front of you all to talk about our beloved grandpa.

Mr. Dan Barnabas, the eldest of our generation, I know it is Dan Moses, but Barnabas is what grandpa named you, so that is how I would prefer to address you. How did it feel to be grandpa's first grandchild? To have all of his love, to go with him into the woods on his bicycle and call it a trip to Greenland? To get neatly dressed up by him, get your shoes polished to his military perfection where you could see your reflection on your shoes?

(Dan trying to hold back his tears with a smile on his face)

I bet you wouldn't trade that privilege to diamonds.

And the gorgeous ladies - Eva, Beauty and Pinky how did you all enjoy it with him? I guess those were the best days of your lives getting spoiled with his love and also being guided through his faith. Would you wish it was any different then? Would you have asked for more?

(Three of them sobbing, faces flushed red. Eva wiping her tears, Beauty holding uptight from bursting out, and Pinky slowly nods no, we couldn't have asked for more)

He was a cool, fun-filled grandpa.

"Love never fails."
Corinthians chapter 13 verse 8

Even before I came into existence, he was long gone,

But he left so much for me to learn,

Speaking of him, I will never be done,

Because there is so much of him in me yet to be born.

So, my love for him would not fail him.

Mom tells me that I am so much like him and he would be so proud if he were alive today.

(Hopeful look at the sky)

He would write lullabies for babies and sing. Once when mom sang one of his songs for me when I was a kid, it flooded my eyes with tears. I still remember the panic I caused saying "I want to meet grandpa". I cried for hours and then passed out.

He probably doesn't even have any idea that I exist, but if he does maybe he will be the happiest today seeing what his little granddaughter has written about him. Not just because he is the loved one, but also because I've inherited his skill of writing too.

I see how painful it is for you all, how there is some piercing pain in your hearts. Might be one of the toughest things you all have ever done. But can we all promise ourselves that we will carry on his legacy of patience, kindness, simplicity, selflessness, forgiveness, standing with the truth, trust, hope, perseverance, and love? Can I get a yes on that, family?

This is our love to the....the heavens grandpa .... we ...we will not fail the love you..... taught us.

It took me all my life to speak here without bursting up. And now as I.... come to an end I can ...no...no longer hold back. (Takes a deep breath to speak clearly)

"The one I love is the one I never met, but also is the one who never leaves." (Trying to control the emotion finishes the talk)

(All the people were sobbing and in tears as I walk back to my seat slowly)

The last enemy to be destroyed will be death.
Corinthians chapter 15 verse 26.

Is it possible to miss someone whom you have no moments or memories with?

You miss.

And sure, your heart mourns for the person.

You might not have memories of the person to miss,

But because you missed making memories with that person.

8

With Love, To the Boss

by Shagabandi Mmanish

The Boss steps in and everyone bows their head to her command. Let me introduce you to this important woman in my life whom my dad once called Kumar Anna for those of you who do not know, Kumar Anna is a Lady Boss kind of a character from a show I don't really remember. Apparently, this Boss of mine is two years elder to me but at times she behaves like she's a decade older but also boss is very much of a child at heart. One could be inspired by her in many ways. One could call her sensitive but she's for sure one of the strongest women I've seen. Her resilience to achieve things is incomparable but that also comes with some stubbornness even for little things like ice cream etc., she wants what she wants.

As I get back from college, freshen up and walk out of my room I see the door of her room is open. I see her scarf on the table and a pair of scrunchies. Those scrunchies which she never allowed me to fidget with because they'd go loose. Does that actually happen? Well, I don't know but all I know is I miss her and if you ask me where she was, she was in Africa to conquer Mount Kilimanjaro. I stand there for a while and go-ahead to pour myself a glass of milk and wish she was with me. I must tell you she actually is boss of the house and I couldn't eat anything delicious till she got back. But that's also the love we have for our Boss.

It has been four days that she's been away from us and I must say I miss working out with her and hogging junk like we never work out. Some of our fond memories lie in this place called Vacs that she loves and loves it even today as an adult. Some things never change you see, especially for people who have a sweet tooth like us. Pani Puri after the gym, who does that? Of course, we do. We both love shawarma. She had her first one with me. Gym and shawarma are like a ritual. Apart from this, this function I attended in her absence made me miss her more.

Whenever she dressed up, she would even make sure that I looked my best too from straightening my hair, to applying foundation on my face. But I do my job too, she makes me click 100 pictures, remains unsatisfied, somehow likes the 150th picture and makes me click some more which according to her should look exactly like what she liked previously or even better and I must say she looks beautiful. We often sat next to each other in functions and family gatherings away from nosy relatives in our world making fun of anything and anyone we see. Ironic but, she's my boss, she presses my shirts and also pressed my uniform during school days. Even today while I work it's the same. Okay, I'll tell you this one incident where it rained heavy, and all the clothes were moist and guess what Boss did? She ironed my boxers and it was hilarious.

Honestly, I find myself very lucky to grow up with a best friend like Boss. We do a lot of comment trolling and I make sure my dear boss is always entertained. I spoke regularly about my lecturers to boss, described them comically and when Boss came along with my parents to a PTM all she did was recollect our conversation and was on the verge of laughing aloud at any moment while making steady eye contact with me. But we got home and laughed our hearts out. I feel boss is very lucky to have such entertainment in her life but also, I am very lucky to have her shoulder to lean on during all lows of my life and celebrate good times too. I must say Boss offers great advice.

Just four days of her absence were enough to walk me down the memory lane while my parents enquired each day if Boss had called, and I shook my head in denial. We all eagerly waited for her call. I never understood why but Boss prefers ringing me up over my parents. I am Boss's favourite I suppose. Suddenly I got a video call from Boss and guess what? She was at 3500 meters height. She was wearing two jackets, gloves, she looked exhausted and was shivering. But there was so much joy in her eyes. Boss was someone who even refused to go to the grocery store with oily hair and look where she was now. That is how passion works I believe. I felt very happy and proud, but my parents felt beyond that as though they were in her place. All of us were so excited that we all spoke at once and in result zero conversation took place. When she called next all of us patiently took turns and spoke to her. It was a moment of extreme joy and pride in our family.

Soon she conquered the highest peak of Africa, Mount Kilimanjaro and made her way back home. By the time she arrived we prepared for a huge celebration, called for a band and a get together with our loved ones. I've known Boss for really long and seeing her passion and love for mountains makes me understand one can do anything with the will to do so. She never let anyone decide what was for her and what was not. She stubbornly achieved most of the things she wanted in life. The universe loves a stubborn heart, and my Boss is the Boss of stubborn hearts, so extra love, I guess. Also, not to forget while she was away and while we danced to the beats of the dhol I thought of her getting married. I thought how I'd dance my heart out in her baraath and miss her, her tantrums, and the omelettes she makes for me. When I speak of tantrums, I must tell you that she makes a baby face whenever she has a craving for ice cream or anything else and I can't deny her request. Oh no! I mean order since she's the Boss. After Mount Kilimanjaro, she didn't stop and went on to conquer two more peaks: Mount Elbrus and Mount Kosciuszko. While everyone advised her to get a job or get married after her engineering, she chose to fulfil her dreams, make us proud and went on to give two ted talks and inspire more people.

Boss becomes Bossier than regular days on Raksha Bandhan. She not only demands her gifts but also demands that I touch her feet and take blessings. Again, this is something that has continued since childhood and I believe will continue even when I become an old man with a backache. While we have a lot of memories together, I'm here trying to share our best ones.

This one time when she had to travel to Srikakulam for training and we travelled together. The bus was moving and we were extremely hungry. The driver did not seem to care about our hunger and stop the bus for dinner. So, we chose to begin hogging. As we unboxed our dinner and began to eat, the aroma of the food spread in the bus and the driver halted the bus exactly in 2 mins. My mum's food had shown its magic is what we thought and laughed. Travelling alone with Boss is fun is what I discovered on that day. Honestly not just travelling but Boss made even boring things fun. For example as kids we had the same home tutor and whenever we found something funny, we would excuse ourselves go to the other room and laugh our ass off. Fun fact Boss was also my senior in school. Boss had this weird phobia of Holi.

She dreaded Holi as a kid but somehow celebrated her first few years ago which I'm proud of. Not to forget that we loved Sankranthi as kids. We both took turns to hold the Chakri as well as fly the kites and blame each other if our kite got cut. It's a memory that is silly, funny and very much loved. This one-time during school when she was an NCC candidate, she stayed away from home in a tent for a week and was missing out on delicious food. The entire week we visited her with her favourite food from Vacs that she used to hog behind her tent escaping anyone's supervision. The memory of her hogging still makes me laugh. While she'd hog, I would find it funny and constantly laugh. She's not just a junk eater but a moody fitness freak too. During the corona lockdown, she chose me to be her trainer (not really) and we helped each other train. By now you must have understood who Boss is – Srujana Shaga aka Daddy's little girl and my beloved sister. Don't ask Mamma's what because I'm Mamma's boy (of course we both are equal but let me have the Mamma's boy title since you are Daddy's little girl).

A huge thank you for all the advice, love, tantrums (I find it cute at times) and sharing your food with me. I promise to share my food, scolding and be there for you all my life irrespective of distance, time, or any circumstances. I love you Akki, don't forget my share in the next chocolate you get. Okay bye!

9

Finally, You Arrived

by Shubha Pai

I woke up in the morning with a jolt, but a happy one. The previous night I couldn't sleep because of the excitement, like a kid one day before his school trip. Today is a very special day. Today is the day when the eyes that I had dreamt of every night will look at me. Today is the day when I will become the reason for the smile that gently spreads across that face. Today is the day that I plan to confess my love. I had been very discreet in expressing my feelings. But today, nobody can stop me. I had waited for this moment for a long time. I don't even know whether it's been hours or days or months. Let me narrate the story of how I fell in love. It started when one day I was awakened from my long sleep. It felt as if someone "opened" me after a long time.

That's when I set my eyes on those eyes that stayed forever in my heart - those eyes that trailed from left to right like a beautiful moving train. The way the lips just curved sometimes in a smile, sometimes in a frown, I have waited long enough to be the reason for that beautiful smile. I waited day and night wondering when those eyes would look at me. Isn't it weird that someone whom I love so ardently doesn't even know of my existence? Well, there are so many lovers with unrequited love whose lover is unaware of their existence, but my love is different. Probably a new kind. I would be bold and even say that the world has never seen such love. It is understandable if you wonder whether this is one of the stalker type love stories that Bollywood has glorified for so many years. But believe me, it's not. I have neither stalked nor have I ever followed my lover like those 'Aashiqs'. There's a long and tiresome rant about Bollywood normalizing stalking in the name of love, but now's not the time for it.

You must be wondering if I've never stalked or silently followed, how am I head over heels in love while my lover doesn't know of my existence. I have stayed for days and months in this exact place that I am now. A lot of people have come and gone but no one till today has caught my attention. I had been waiting for the day when I would get the attention I had given and here finally, the day has arrived.

Firstly, you must realise the hard work it takes to confess love. It's not as easy as they show in books or tv series or movies. It takes a lot of courage and especially for someone like me in such a situation. It takes more than a stem of rose, more than a ring of love and more than the strain of kneeling down on one knee. I know at this point, you will roll your eyes and exclaim, "Seriously? Just do it, bro. It's not that big a deal." Well, easy for you to say. You are either one of those privileged people who've been proposed before or someone who has done it boldly and even succeeded. Many people think that the fear of rejection is what stops many people from confessing. For me, it's not that. At this point most of you might be thinking, "Point pe aa na Bhai. I'm sure it's one of those 'out – of -my – league kind stories". Well, if you ask me, there's nothing out-of-my-league for anyone in this world.

That's the thing with love, it's always been in-the-league.

The hard truth is the identity of my lover, for some, it might come as a shock, while for some it might come as a sweet surprise, but I hope that the final outcome will be my lover's smile. You, my lover, have finally arrived today to read my confession. Yes, you. The one who is reading this while I confess, it's you, the reader who bought this book and started reading it. It's always been you. You can take your time to go back to the start of this story and read it again to be sure whether it's you. I will wait here as you read it again. (It's not a new thing you see, I had waited till you read all the previous stories)

If you're wondering why I fell in love with you, there are a lot of reasons. Well, you love books, and you love reading. That makes one huge point for why I love you. The way you opened the cover eager to read it, that was the time when you woke me up and I fell in love with those eyes. The excitement in your eyes to read new stories, that smile that swept across your face when you read something relatable, the way you rolled your eyes while reading something cheesy, the way you smiled after every story, the way you're blushing now. Aren't these reasons enough to make me fall in love with you? Every time you faced a problem, you ended up facing it with courage.

It could be any problem from losing someone special or scoring low in an exam or trying hard to convince your parents for something. You never gave up. Even when you did, you made sure you kept that hope alive inside you and that made you so human. For every time you made someone smile, for every time you wished a stranger "Good morning," for every time you said "thank you" to the shopkeeper, you made me fall in love with you. It's not like I've not thought this through. I had been thinking about this for long hours and had even discussed it with a friend of mine. Sri Charan, from Manish's story, (if you haven't read his story yet, you should!) asked me not to confess my love. He said that my love would never be reciprocated. I said, "Isn't it better that way?"

It wasn't the fear of rejection that was stopping me from confessing, rather it was the fear of acceptance. What if you like me? I'm a mere character of a short story in an anthology but you gave me life. You could have chosen any other book, but you chose this book, you chose to read this story and you chose to fall in love with me. Oh c'mon, don't tell me you've not fallen for me already. At this point, you are smirking at me and thinking, "Don't you think you're a little overconfident?" Well, who is not? But again, as I said, I am open for rejection. If you do not like me, it's completely fine. I understand the idea of consent even though I'm just a character. I realise many of my ancestors had not quite understood the concept of consent, and I apologise for that.

You understand now why my love story is different from others? My love is weird, it's silly, it's funny, it's even impossible, but it's true and pure. I love you as much as any lover has ever loved or maybe even more because I exist because of you. What is a character without its reader but a mere product of fiction? This is a love story between two worlds – your world where everything is so busy with motion and my world where everything is just words until it's read. On one hand, your world is real but horrific, on the other hand, my world is fictional but beautiful. How I wish to bring you to my world, but it's not possible. I can never have the courage to enter your world. So, I guess, this is how it's supposed to be. I will be here waiting for you, every time you open the book. If you're wondering how I look, just close your eyes, and form a picture of me. Yes, that's exactly how I look. Don't go by the face of my author, I'm not her. I'm just a fragment of her imagination.

Whenever you feel worthless, just remember that there's someone who loves you for who you are. I will always be here to make you smile. If you're feeling low, you can always hug me and fall asleep. I'm happy as long as I don't end up in a 'bhelpuri' bandi holding bhel. Even if I do and you end up reading this page, you should try getting the book.

On a serious note, I'm glad we crossed paths. If not for you, I would not never see the light of the day (quite literally). It took a lot of courage for me to confess this love, this love that is impossible but yet was inevitable. You became the lens through which I could see your world. The vision was so beautiful that even in a world like yours, I could see goodness and beauty. There's one thing about stories that people don't realise. By reading stories, you help the characters fulfil their purpose as they help you live different lives. You've fulfilled my purpose and so have I by helping you live a different life. But have I really? This story is about you, my love. I have just reminded you to live your life through this story, through my love.

You must understand how different my confession is from conventional love confessions. What I have for you is purely platonic. It's like the love shared between a mother and a child. It's the love shared by siblings and friends. Now you understand why it is inevitable. It's just about the connection, you see. You might be a man, a woman or a queer. You might be straight or anyone belonging to the pride community. I love you, no matter what because you chose to read my story among the rest. You chose this book among all the other books in your cart or the shelf. You chose me among several other characters.

Why have I confessed now, you might be wondering. Well, you might be someone who has a loving family and dotting friends, or you might be someone who is questioning your self-worth. That's why I'm here. I'm here to remind you on all your low days that there is still hope. I'm here to remind you that you're okay by yourself too. Love should only strengthen oneself and make one realise one's self-worth. If it snatches away your identity, makes you bound to duties and responsibilities, forces you to compromise, what's the use of such love. Katrina Kaif in Ajab Prem ki Ghazab Kahani says, "Books na humare Sache dost hote hai. Na complaints na demands bas saath deti hai". Well, I'm a book too and that's what I plan to do.

Just like this, I confess my feelings to you. I love you, my reader. You don't know it but you're someone who deserves happiness. You're beautiful inside out and you deserve to be loved. My heart feels light now, it feels as if some weight has been lifted from my chest. The secret that I had hidden for such a long time is out now. Now that finally, you arrived.

10

The Apology

by Rosalind Princess Reshma

I f not for the foul stench of garbage, he would've believed it was a dream. Returning from his evening walk, he had stopped to buy cigarettes. The ancient-looking shop was the closest to the spooky house that was to be his home for quite some time. The shopkeeper, a man who looked as ancient as the shop, was curious. Strangers always attracted attention in a small town. The old man was about to pour out his questions when she arrived. She knew what she wanted; Tomatoes, onions, half a kg each, and garlic and ginger, three each. Yes, you heard it right. No, not the paste. Also, a bunch of dhania. That's it… Sagar didn't have to look at her to know that it was her. Her voice hadn't changed. Judging from what she was buying, neither had her habits. She was going to cook khichdi for dinner, her only solid meal of the day. She didn't bargain. She paid him the exact change and left. She didn't look around. Had she turned to her left; she would've seen him. But, what if she had? It would've been awkward.

He felt silly. Friends drifted apart and reunited all the time. When you see a long-lost friend after ages, you go to them and talk about how times have changed. You don't try to wish them away. Only people who do not want to revisit their past do that. He wasn't one of them. He was a very nostalgic person.

He was tempted to follow her, and he took two steps towards her. She stopped abruptly. He knew why. She had spotted a plastic cover on the road. She bent down to pick it up and she caught him staring at her. If she was surprised, she didn't show it. She got up, walked to the other side of the road, and dumped the plastic cover on a heap of garbage. She didn't turn around to look at him again. She walked on. He was disappointed. He hoped she would notice him and begin a conversation so he wouldn't have to take the effort.

Ideally, he should have thought about the first day at kindergarten when a girl with mismatched ribbons on her pigtails decided to give him her candy because he had been crying uncontrollably. Or he should have remembered one of those numerous times she had saved him from his parents' wrath by assuring them that the test had been, in fact, very tough and that the whole class had failed the test. She had been a pillar of support, the keeper of his secrets. Surprisingly, the first memory that surfaced that evening was not of their first meeting. It was one of those obscure ones which one is not aware of having till they flood back abruptly...

"Isn't it high time they stop teaching Shakespeare?" she was ranting.

They were returning from the library. She with a bunch of books on feminism, contemporary poetry, and the history of Indian writing in English, and he with his copy of The Prelude for the next day's presentation. He had no idea why she was talking about Shakespeare all of a sudden. They did not have to study Shakespeare that term.

"And teach what? Only Chaucer and Milton?" he had retorted.

"I say, stop everything. Enough of Chaucer, Milton, and Shakespeare. English Literature should be more…contemporary."

"Like what, Medhya?"

"Like translated….well, leave it… You know what? There shouldn't be an English Literature department. Just Literature departments. Only then we can move on…"

"Now you are being too idealistic."

"I'm not. I'm just saying we should be taught how to create works of art rather than keep analysing the same old ones again and again. At this point we are appreciating works of literature, just dissecting them. Also, I hate Shakespeare."

He wanted to laugh, but he didn't. It would taint his 'studious guy' image. Studious guys were supposed to be serious and serious people never laughed. Not in public. He just wished she would stop ranting. She did. Soon enough. Her smile brightened a little more and she closed her eyes, facing the sky.

"Did you feel that?" she asked.

"What?"

"It's going to rain, Sagar. I felt a drop on my face."

"Then we better get back to the library and wait till it stops…or just rush, before it starts getting heavy…"

"It's too late for that, sir." She said, sticking out her tongue at him.

She was right. It had started raining.

"I have an umbrella." He told her calmly.

"Which we don't need now."

"Are you out of your mind? It's raining and we are carrying books. Books borrowed from the library, ma'am."

She winked and pointed at her bag.

"It's waterproof. Now give me your book."

She stuffed it in along with her books and looked up.

"There's a solution to everything, Sagar. Now, we are going to enjoy a walk in the rain. I know you have never done it before."

He had no option.

"I can't believe I'm doing this!" he said, to no one in particular.

"Don't tell me you aren't enjoying it."

He wanted to tell her that he wasn't. He was feeling cold and 'nasty'. That's how he would've described the day. Nasty. But there was a tiny part of him that was feeling good. He couldn't lie to her.

"Okay…I agree, it does feel good, but both of us are going to fall sick."

"We can take medicines and some rest. We'll be fine."

"Look at our clothes, Medhya! We can build a hut with all that mud."

"Clothes can be washed. If you can't afford a detergent, I'll give you one."

"You have an answer for everything, don't you?"

She laughed. That poking, irritating laughter of hers!

"Sagar, if I die tonight, I don't want to die with the regret that I could have walked in the rain but didn't."

That was the Medhya he knew. The woman who wanted to live without regrets. The woman who was stupid, impulsive, and happy, and had managed to brush off a little of her stupidity, impulsiveness, and happiness on him. Just a little. And the woman he was looking at was a stranger. She looked different. She wasn't exactly melancholic, but she did not look like someone who would jump into a puddle.

But then she had always been the mature one though her actions made it look otherwise. Sure, she would walk in the rain and fight over that last slice of pizza, but she was also the person who told him that marks did not decide someone's worth when he had failed an examination for the first time. She had helped him pick a gift for his ninth-grade crush- the most popular boy in school. She hadn't judged him. She hadn't even made him feel 'different'. When the rest of the world saw him as a criminal for not being into girls 'like a normal boy', she was his safe place. And he had single-handedly demolished that safe place.

Of course, betraying her had never been his intention. But it happened and he could never muster up the courage to apologise.

He had always wanted to be a writer. Telling stories was his gift, or so he believed until he hit a writer's block that lasted three years. The success of his first book just set the bar too high for his second...of which he hadn't written more than three pages. Just when he thought he could give up; he remembered a conversation he had had with Medhya long ago. She had tried her hand at writing at some point and given up. Her ideas had been good, but she was not good with words. Which is why she had asked for his help. She had written a story about a mysterious unmarked grave and a series of shocking revelations. It was poorly written and too prosaic. She had asked him to read it and help her rewrite it, but he had kept procrastinating till it was forgotten.

Suddenly, that half-written story became his saviour. He barely worked on it for a week before sending it to the publisher. He did not expect it to be loved by his readers. It was supposed to be filler so that he would have enough time to create his next masterpiece. But destiny had other plans and before he knew it, he was the next bestselling author. Medhya was not stupid. She just had to read the synopsis to know that he had stolen her story. He did not want to face her...and so he left...

That was a decade ago. He had almost forgotten about it. All the years of pretending the story were his, had somehow convinced him that there was no need to feel guilty. But then he had never thought he would run into her like this...

He watched her walking as if the world around her didn't exist. Another step, or maybe two, and she would disappear around the corner. But she stopped. Before he could make out what was happening, she turned back and started walking, all the way back. When she came close to him, he didn't move. Now he saw a trace of anger on her face. Before he could speak, she snatched the cigarette from his hand, threw it on the ground, stamped on it and without speaking a word, turned back and walked away. There was a chance of atonement. There was still hope...

He ran towards her. The slope made it difficult and when he stopped to catch his breath, he realized he had grown old. She was fast but he caught up with her.

"Medhya," he said, panting. "Do you remember me?"

It was a stupid question. He realized that as soon as the words left his mouth. But then what else could he have asked her? Would you like to slap me for the idiot I have been? Or, hello there, we used to be best friends till I stooped low and betrayed you for fame?

She did not stop but slowed down. She did not look at him.

"Of course, I do," she replied. "How have you been?"

There was no anger. No sarcasm. She genuinely wanted to know how he was doing, and he did not know what to say to that.

"Not bad, I guess." he managed to say.

"That's good, for a popular person like you."

Again, it was just a statement. No implications.

"So, what are you doing here?" when she spoke again, he became conscious of the awkward silence that preceded it.

"Research. My next book is about a murder in a small town...so..."

He regretted saying it.

"That's nice." she meant it.

"So, you live here?" he knew small talk was not going to fix what his mistake had damaged, but it was worth trying.

"Yes, we moved here three years ago. You see that restaurant there? My husband's family has owned it for ages, and he wanted to renovate it...so… Anyway, you should drop in someday. You'd like the food."

"I would love to."

It would be someday. The conversation was over. She probably had somewhere to be.

"It was nice meeting you," he said, feebly.

She looked at him and smiled.

"Come on, say it," she said, with a smile.

"What?" he knew what she meant but he did not know how to apologise.

"I can see that something has been bothering you. You just abruptly stopped talking to me all those years ago. I have often wondered how I might have offended you, but I have never understood. And now, you are behaving like we were never best friends. Just acquaintances who...drifted apart. I have the right to know. What did I do?"

Was she kidding? Didn't she know that it wasn't she who had done something wrong but him? Did she not know? And then it struck him. Of course, she didn't.

"I owe you an apology." he began. "An apology will not change anything but it's the right thing to do."

She looked confused.

"I shouldn't have stolen your idea." he continued. "I knew it was wrong and I did it anyway. I was desperate. I was not in a position to return the advance...I needed the money... Anyway, none of that justifies what I did. It was your story, and I stole it. I did not even mention you in the acknowledgements and I understand if you can't forgive me. But I am sorry. I am."

He knew she would forgive him. She would say something about things being water under the bridge and everything would be fine.

"What?" she exclaimed and burst out laughing, to his surprise. "You thought I would be upset so you stopped talking to me? You are dumb! You're still so dumb!"

She paused to laugh again.

"Why do you think I shared that idea with you?" she asked

him, still laughing.

"Because you wanted my help to write it?" he suggested.

"No, idiot. I wanted you to write it. It was a good idea, and I knew you would do justice to it...and from what I see, you have."

There was a brief silence and then he began to laugh too.

"So, are you telling me I was feeling guilty for ten years for absolutely no reason?"

"Yup."

And then he realized. His best friend was still the same person. She had not changed. Just grown-up. What he thought was bitterness, was, in fact, contentment. He was looking at the face of a woman who had no regrets so far. And he could feel some of that contentment and happiness rubbing off on him.

11

A Modern Day Fairytale

by Anshika Prem Chhattani

In a land far far away, there once lived a King.

King Ibrahim Zafar. The king always wanted a son who would take care of his kingdom after he was gone. Soon enough, the King had a child. Everyone in the Kingdom started calling the child "Adi".

Adi was the kind of child, every other person in the Kingdom wished for. Brown eyes, short silky hair, a smile so innocent and pure that could melt anyone's heart in a second. Adi's nature was the biggest asset, filled with so much kindness and generosity. Adi could never see anyone crying and was always there to help people out.

As a child, Adi loved reading novels and writing poems. But a warrior never reads. The warrior should master the art of sword fighting. "The pen is mightier than the sword" was not true in Adi's case. The day came when the pen was soon replaced with a sword and Adi was made to be ready for the battlefield. Every time, seeing Adi practice, the King always felt that Adi was not yet ready for the battlefield. Day in and day out of vigorous training, Adi still couldn't satisfy the King.

Every time something used to seem missing, something that made King believe that Adi was yet not ready.

Times changed. Soon troubles started brewing in the Kingdom. There were clouds of darkness surrounding the Palace. The Mughals had raised war against the King's Dynasty. They claimed that the land the King's Palace was built on was theirs and they were here to win it back. If not returned to them they would raise a war against them. The King's worst nightmare came true. The last time the King went on a war against the Mughals, he had lost his first wife. His first love. They could never have a child but that didn't change the love the King had for his first wife. The King could've gone through anything to save his first wife, but he couldn't. He couldn't win the battle and thus his wife lost her life.

This was the King's biggest fear. He couldn't find a way out to save his Kingdom. All the memories came rushing down the memory lane and his wounds were fresh. The King decided that he didn't want to raise war and he would give away the land to the Mughals. Adi couldn't bear this. The thought of giving up even before trying was not something that was taught. Adi went to the King's room and tried convincing the King to fight and not give in just like that. But to no avail, the King was firm on his decision.

The day of the war came. As the King went on the battlefield to surrender, to his surprise he saw Adi backing him up with the army. Adi was firm and confident and determined to not give up this time. "I cannot abort without trying, that would be a pity," said Adi.

The King knew the scars of the previously lost battle had left an invisible but permanent mark on his life. He knew what it was to live with being called a failure. And he wouldn't choose this fate for Adi. In the previous battle, the King not only lost his wife but also his army, and the land his ancestors had left for him.

King ordered Adi, "I will not allow you to waste your life in pursuit of something that is not possible. Something so materialistic in nature. Hope is a dangerous thing and seeing your performance, I don't have that either. You are not quite ready yet. There's a lot for you to learn."

Adi pleaded to the king "You've always been my inspiration. I look up to you for all the big fights in my life and even today I'm looking to you. I want to fight once for your father. I don't want to give up on my dream. On your dream. Winning the battle against the Mughals has always been your dream. The biggest dream of your life which you couldn't fulfil. I've only seen one dream ever since I was born, that is to fulfil your dream." with eyes full of tears.

King just kept staring at Adi. He was speechless.

Adi continued with tears in eyes, "I want to try again father. And I'm not afraid of falling again. I'll learn to live with the scars of failure but not with the scar of giving up. I won't be able to face myself or meet my eyes in the mirror, knowing that I gave up easily. I gave up even before trying. I'm okay being a stagnant lake if you're my ocean."

The war happened because Adi was determined to not let the King give up this time. There were bodies lashed out. Bloodshed everywhere, people died, there were clouds of danger surrounding the battlefield. Swords tangling with each other. The King got injured and was sent back to the Palace because being on the battlefield would only bring him one thing and that was death.

The war went on for a few hours, the sun came down,

slowly, the day turned into evening and evening into the night. The war was over. The winner was declared.

The messenger of the Kingdom entered. There were colours of happiness everywhere. People were dancing out of joy. Because the war was won. The King got his territory back. His kingdom back. Along with the news followed another news by one of the army men.

The news was that Adi was no more. Adi lost the life given to see the King live.

Adi lost but the war was not lost. How could the King lose the war when his daughter was holding the sword. A flood of emotions came inside the King.

The King found a letter in Adi's room. The envelope read, "To be read when I'm gone!"

The King opened the letter with trembling hands and read:

Dear Father,

I might have not been the daughter you always wanted me to be but trust me I've always tried. I've tried my level best. And I promise you to be that daughter that makes you proud in every phase of my life. You never said, "I am proud of you" and that's okay because I'm not going anywhere, unless and until I don't hear it from you! I will not stop unless you don't hug me, kiss my forehead, and say it to me that you're proud of me. I promise to keep you in my heart and in every step that I take towards life. You've taught me so much in life that I can never thank you enough for. In every phase, you were as strong as a pillar. I might've not seen you holding my back, but I know you were there. Silent but Strong! You taught me that it's in our hand how we tell our story to the world. We can be a victim to it, or we can come out of it stronger as a survivor. And I surely am a Survivor because I am your daughter." Father, you've held parts of me that would've shattered, had you not been there. You didn't let me fall, and if I ever did, you made sure I was on my feet again. I hope that one day, you both will be proud in knowing that I made it. I made it where I wanted to. I want you to know that I'll always be incomplete without you and as long as I have you and these wings that you gave me, I don't need anyone else to help fly! And now that I am gone, I don't want you to stop like a stagnant lake, I want you to flow like a river and never stop until one day you meet your ocean.

Your Adi

King wept as he read the letter. She was his ocean. The King remembered how much she loved reading and how 'PS I Love You' was her favourite book. The next day, the King visited the cemetery with his daughter's favourite book. His heart was flooded with emotions and he knew what he would say to his daughter when the clouds break away. His daughter was not a deserter, she was a warrior.

"In the loving memory of Aditi Ibrahim Zafar,

A magnificent warrior and a loving daughter"

Is what the tombstone read!

12

Untitled

by Johnny Pasapala

It was a few weeks into my first year of college, I was walking out of the class at a slow pace, wondering why my day ended so fast. But everybody rushed out in a second as if they've been waiting for it to get over. I slowly raised my head and saw a huge crowd of strangers and a few familiar faces here and there, walking along with me out of the campus. I made it till the gate with an empty face looking around to see if there was someone, I could speak to among the scattered groups of students outside the college gate. Luckless; I walked through the mass towards the road where people waited for the Auto Rickshaws. The college was around a kilometre away from the bus stop, and I used to take an Autorickshaw to reach there. I stood there looking at Autos coming and going for a while until I decided to walk. I was not the only one, there were groups of people walking before and after… but I was the only one walking alone. I realized that I liked walking, it saved me some money and gave me some time to think about my day. So, I started walking every day.

On one of those, while I walked out of college, I saw someone I knew from my class walking right behind me. I paused while he looked at me and caught up. He asked me where I live and I said, "Medchal." He gently nodded and I asked him the same and he said something I couldn't catch, I asked for his pardon, he said with a steady voice, "Bowenpally." I looked at him and smiled. Our conversation continued until we reached the bus stop, and we parted our ways. The next day after college, I saw him again and we began to walk together. He asked me why I walked alone every day, I told him how I always liked being alone, watching things happen from a distance. He, with a rather solicitous voice, said, "Don't walk alone." That was something people seldom told me.

I was from a small city called Vijayawada. I lived there for as long as I could remember, I changed four different schools, but I never managed to make a friend. When I entered high school, people started to bully me. I hated my school life and always wanted to leave. Every day after school hours, I ran back home and climbed up the terrace of our apartment complex and stared at the highway going north. I spent most of my time there while other kids were downstairs playing cricket. I could see the Krishna river, far away, on the other side of the highway. The only thing that defined my teenage self was my love for the sky.

When I was sixteen, I had just taken my secondary school exams, my dad told us that we're moving to Hyderabad. He hoped to give my sister and me more opportunities and space to grow. I was excited… anticipating a fresh start and a clean slate. But I was rather startled when I came here, people spoke differently, lived differently, everything was dull and prompt. I hated it. I stubbornly rejected every junior college application my dad brought to me. I resisted until one day he forced me into joining a college close to my house where people treated me like I was some alien. So, I had to spend most of my childhood alone.

When He told me to not walk alone, I was befuddled. I did not know why he said that…

I kept telling him all my school stories and family trips, and he just listened to me. He listened to me so keenly like no one ever did before. One day, I was in the middle of telling him about my favourite TV show, we reached the bus stop… but he kept walking towards a bench beside the bus stop under a tree and we sat there till I completed my story. We soon made it our routine, walking every day after college, sitting on that bench, letting our days out, and him listening to me like I'm his favourite song. We sat there while the dusk consumed the sky and the streetlights flashed. We watched the buses come by people getting in and out of the buses… and days went by so fast.

I articulated every single event of my life when I was with him. I rarely looked into his eyes when I spoke, but when I did, I saw him captivated with me like I'm a piece of art. I felt my darkness unbind; I faced my biggest fears… I felt liberated.

I have a thing for voices. when I like someone's voice, it's stuck in my head forever. His voice…although he rarely spoke, anything he said was steady. His voice was sparkling, he slightly dragged the last part of my name every time he said it; I found that quite amiable. He had this unusual charm… a vibe quite agreeable and jolly. I observed him around in college. Everybody liked him, they found him quite intriguing just like I did. I smiled more; I smiled at him, I smiled at the thought of him… I smiled at everyone around me.

A few weeks later, we walked back to our bench, sat there

waiting for a bus. We rested our feet on the railing that divided the footpath and the road. His shoes were beside mine; I pulled my phone out and took a picture. He suddenly tapped my shoulder and pointed at a bus coming our way…I looked back at him saying, "Which bus is it!? I can't see".

"Why can't you see? You have your glasses on".

"Yeah, but I think my sight has changed now… these glasses are pretty old you know."

He stared at my glasses. I felt awkward. He slowly reached out to my face and removed my glasses. Everything went instantly blurry; I could only see him. He observed them for a few seconds and tsk-ed under his breath. He pulled out a handkerchief from his pocket and firmly held my glasses between his fingers while he cleaned them. He raised them to his eye level to check if they were clean enough and handed them to me saying, "Check now." I put them back on and tried to look at the road… my eyes widened; I was stunned. everything looked crystal clear, almost like I was in a different place altogether. I looked at him with a wide smile and said, "Oh my god, Thank you!" He subtly smiled and asked me if I could see the bus number now, I nodded in agreement, looking at him. His smile widened a bit and said, "you should clean them more often". We both laughed and completely forgot about the bus.

We always forgot about the bus; our purpose sitting at the bus stop was never to go home. On weekends, we hung out till it was very late. Every time my bus came, he would look at me to see if I got in; I would smile and say 'next bus' but it was never the next one. I secretly kept a count of all the 'next buses' and on some days, it went as high as thirty. I always wondered if he wanted me to go … he knew all he had to do is leave. But he never left and neither did I.

I was quite a spoilt child if not just sad. My first day at college was also my first day taking a bus. On that very day, I also realized that the bus drivers do not stop the bus completely at your stop but only slow it down to almost zero and expect you to get down the moving bus. Me being the noob I am, fell flat on my face (literally), attempting that. When I told him this story, he laughed aloud like a kid. I frowned at his insensitivity, but then he started explaining physics…he said, "You feel because you tried to get down perpendicular to the bus, like as if the bus was still." I was confused… He further explained inertia, speed, and inconsistency of force which sounded like Chinese to me. I hate science but he loved it… He later insisted on giving me a demonstration. He held my hand, pulled me into a bus that was at the stop. we both got in and he said, "I'll show you how to do it in the next stop."

"No way! I'm not breaking my arm at the expense of your stunt", I protested.

He stood calmly on the steps of the bus door; his hair slightly blew in the wind. He smiled at me and said, "This is not a stunt. This is a life skill."

The bus approached the next stop. I began to feel my feet getting cold. I said, "I can't do this."

"You can! Just follow me."

He banged against the outside of the bus, indicating to the driver to stop. The bus slowed down ... He hung precariously from the pole beside the door, holding the pole with one hand. I held my breath as he put one leg forward and took a leap on one leg, in the direction of the moving bus, and then began running comfortably along with the bus. He then gestured to me to do the same, and said: "C'mon, now you do it!" As the bus slowed down further, I took a nervous step down the steps of the bus and gulped down my fear. I put my left foot forward first, managing an unsteady jump, followed by a slow run to catch up with the speeding bus .... Gradually, I was able to catch a comfortable pace, while I was still gasping when I heard his voice behind me saying, 'See, you did it!"

I looked up and he was running to me, smiling. He came and hugged me while I was still catching my breath. Later that day, I had my first shawarma ever, with him to celebrate my little achievement.

He taught me to read a clock, he taught me to use Snapchat, and most importantly, he taught me to open up.

When I opened up, I became more sociable. I was not the silent kid who walked alone anymore. I had definite taste; an image to keep up. So, I naturally made new friends and all my friends were his friends too. We had a circle, there were new people with us. Well, I felt like they came between us. All of us certainly had fun but it wasn't as fun. Something was different, something was changing…

One day, I waited for him outside the college. But he never showed up, he didn't take my calls. I assumed that he was busy and left for home… Someone told me that they saw him walking to the bus stop that day. I did not want to take it seriously; he had his own life. But later that night, things started adding up in my head. We had a long weekend because of a cyclone. So, I decided to wait until the next week to ask him about it.

My Monday blues were dense; He did not come to college that day. I called him up after classes and he said he'd meet me at our spot. I liked the weather; it was drizzling. I decided to walk. I strolled on the muddy grass verge of the road, listening to my footsteps slimy splashing mud, contemplating whether I should ask him about what I heard; it kept me sleepless after all. I wondered if he replaced me, I wondered if he didn't care about me anymore. When I reached the bus stop, he was on his phone, sitting on our bench. I walked towards him on the pavement while I closed my umbrella. He looked up towards me and said in a rather furious tone, "Did you walk alone?" I smiled and said, "Yes, sir." I forgot everything I had in mind when I heard his voice. I sat beside him and waited for him to say something, but he was on his phone the whole time. we did not say a word to each other. I still felt comfortable in his silence. He never mentioned his little exploration to me, but his silence spoke it through. Thereafter, we ignored each other, I did most, and he just went along.

I never wanted to move on, but I had to… from how he avoided me I thought he wanted me to. The summer break was on, I went back to my hometown visiting my extended family; they all were surprised at how much I had to say about everything. It made sense. But, if it weren't for my parents insisting on me, I never would have spoken or visited them at all, but now I liked speaking to people. Although, they were still nosy about my unconventional preferences and opinions.

Our old house looked different; I stood at that same spot on the rooftop staring at the Krishna river. All those memories glanced at me at the moment. I realized how much I had changed.

I came back home but I seldom thought about him. We did not speak all summer. He did not come to college on the first day and I never bothered why. People asked me why he wasn't coming to college and I dully said, "I don't know". I walked back to the bus stop that day; for old times' sake, I thought. It was a sunny day. The sound of my footsteps slightly annoyed me, so I plugged in my earphones and listened to music for the rest of the way. Johnny Cash sang in my ears, "Please don't take my sunshine away…"

As I approached the bus stop, my eyes were automatically drawn to that green concrete bench. I walked towards it as if something pulled me there. It was empty, I walked closer and took a seat. Slowly resting my feet on the railing. I took a deep breath and felt the breeze run through my hair. I paused the music on my phone, pulled my earphones out and kept them aside. I closed my eyes, trying to not think about something in particular. I heard dried leaves rustling… they crackled as someone walked on them, I tried to ignore it. Gradually, I heard some footsteps approaching, my heart started beating heavily. I slowly opened my eyes and turned to my side. And there He was…

13

My Wonder Woman

by Aishwarya K

Family and family ties are the core of every society. They are essential for a society to grow and prosper in the long and short run. I might sound like a sociology professor, but we often disregard the significance of strong family ties. Every family member from our uncles and aunts to grandparents and cousins, apart from parents and siblings, are essential in guiding us. I am going to tell you about the most valuable member of my family that I have come to respect as Wonder Woman.

Out of everyone in my family, I have never wholly appreciated the bond I have with my maternal grandmother. She is my wonder woman. My ammamma, as we call a grandmother, was a very disciplined and authoritative person. If not for her advanced age, I would have said that she still is authoritative. She held the entire family and extended family under a strong edict for many a year, not in a 'godfather' kind of way. She is a principled person, who stood by her beliefs and made sure her family followed them as well. She was a tough nut to crack and would not be influenced by bullies. With her temperament and disposition, she motivated the family while instilling the strength to carry on.

Today, I will speak about my relationship with her and what I have learnt from her. To start, I was in awe of her as a child and loved her just like most kids love their grandparents. As I grew older, playing with my cousins and getting up to mischief became my primary focus. My interactions with her were limited to chastisement and punishment. During my summer vacations, she would find innovative ways to correct us without being harsh. One day, all of us children were especially unruly, and we caused mayhem in the house during playtime. The punishment we received that day was the most memorable one, not because of the severity, but for its simplicity. As punishment, ammamma made all of us eat plain curd and rice, while the rest of the family ate delicious prawn curry. She wanted to show us that good children get tasty food and bad ones eat boring food. As we were kids, that was a very powerful message that became ingrained in our brain. All her punishments were harmless, but memorable in some way or the other.

One summer, we went out for a picnic and ended up eating a lot of junk food along the way. As kids, we made use of our collective powers of persuasion. Speaking, we threw a tantrum and managed to blackmail the elders to get us all the street food that we wanted. Of course, it was not healthy food, and we would have most likely fallen sick if not for my grandma. She punished us by making us drink castor oil when we came back home. It tasted awful and we hated it. What we did not know was that it was a powerful laxative that cleared out the digestive tract and washed all the infections out of the system.

There was another instance when my grandma taught us patience. She would tell us stories every afternoon, about faraway kingdoms with handsome princes and magical creatures. I never realized it at that time, but all her stories had a very strong theme of bravery, integrity, and righteous behaviour. She would weave these values into her stories and made us believe in them as well. One summer afternoon, she told us the 'Apoorva Chintamani Katha'. It was a particular favourite of all the kids and my grandma brought the story to an interesting turn and stopped. She said that she had a lot of work and could not spare time for stories. All of us were distraught and planned to help her finish the work fast so that we can get to hear the story. That year, she taught us how to make pickles, sun-dried fryums, and even taught us how to bake a cake to celebrate our success, before finishing the story. She used the same tactic to teach us crochet, knitting, and needlework the following summer.

As we grew, the style of her stories changed from magical to more realistic ones. They were more relatable to everyday life but had a strong message, nonetheless. She got me hooked on the children's magazine, Chandamama and taught me how to read Telugu. I remember one story of hers that I only understand now. The true impact of the story has dawned on me only after seeing a similar scenario in real-life. This made my memories of her stories even more valuable. The story goes as follows:

There once was a small village in the outskirts of a big kingdom. Since the village was in the outskirts of the kingdom, most of the welfare efforts of the king did not reach this village. The villagers had long ago learnt to be self-sufficient. In this village was a young lad named Gopal, who was respectful of elders, law-abiding, and conscientious. He was ready to help anyone in need and was the first one to offer assistance. His helping nature and courteous behaviour became legendary in not just his village, but also the nearby villages. Everyone would come directly to the young lad with requests to get their work done.

Slowly, as time passed, the young lad was not young anymore. As Gopal started to age, the demands of the people around him started to feel burdensome. The stress of keeping up this attitude started to take a toll on his health. He was forced to refuse to help others and it hurt him to see the disappointment in the faces of the villagers.

Over time, some villagers recognized the effort it was taking Gopal to do simple tasks. They wanted to help him with his tasks and responsibilities. But, as they say, "A hand that helps does not like to take help." When the youngsters in the village tried to help Gopal and share his burden, Gopal felt insulted. He saw their help as an affront to his failing health. He misunderstood their affection as pity. He became aggressive and overexerted himself. He pushed away any help that came his way and scowled at the youngsters who offered to help.

One day a learned and wise Swamiji visited the village. Everyone in the village visited him to pay their respects and take his advice on the different problems they face. Gopal also visited him and spoke of his problem. The wise Swamiji immediately recognised the actual problem. The problem was not the attitude of the villagers or Gopal's failing health. It was his ego. He made Gopal aware of this fact. He advised Gopal to put himself in the shoes of the youngsters and look at his situation before judging them. He made Gopal realise that everyone ages and with their age, people should learn to adjust to the changes in relationship dynamics. Rather than feeling left out or obsolete, one should reinvent their role as a mentor or guide. Gopal could befriend the youngsters and teach them about his experiences and pass his wisdom on to them rather than considering them as competition.

When ammamma told me this story, I found it odd that the wise man asked Gopal to give up. However, after reaching my age, I can see the wisdom in that advice. We often come across situations at our workplace, where the old and senior employees complain about the attitude and work culture of the new and younger employees. I was able to handle a few confrontations better because of these lessons I have learnt. My grandma was not only preparing me to adjust with our ageing process, but she was also helping us adjust with her advancing age. She was teaching us to take over the baton from her hands. Such was her wisdom and foresight.

At this point, I would also like to throw some light on my grandma's early years. While speaking to my mother, I asked her about my ammamma, and I found that she was a very forward-thinking and open-minded person. Before I share any of her anecdotes, I would like you to remember that this was the pre-independence era. My ammamma always wanted to have daughters and she was blessed with 3 sons before my mother was born. Since my grandfather was from a poor family, she felt that her children will not get the same respect as her other affluent relatives. So, she made sure all her children were well educated, including her daughters. At a time when child marriages were common, ammamma insisted that my mother married only after reaching 18 years. She enrolled my mother in a convent school and taught her piano and violin. She also taught her classical Indian music just so she does not lose touch with Indian heritage.

She tried to do the same with my aunts as well, however, they were not musically inclined. They were convent educated and completed their degree before marriage. She made sure all her daughters were married into educated families. She was also very open-minded about women's rights. She never backed away from standing up for her fellow women though they were ostracised by the rest of the community. She opened up her house to everyone who asked for help and proved their good intentions. She had more control over her son's friends than their own family, because of her strong will and sturdy ideals. To this day, when they visit my uncles, they seek my ammamma's blessing and spend time with her.

I have other interesting facts about her and my paternal grandmother. Both my grandmothers were neighbours and fast friends before they realised they were related. Later, of course, they solidified their bond with the marriage of my parents. Anyway, back in the day when both my grandmothers were friends, they would plan out ways to navigate the social circles. They helped other women in our community by gathering support and strengthening their voice without offending elders of the family. They would sit out in front of the house while eating fruits and discussing family politics and difficult 'in-laws'. They would plan home economics and help each other out with budget deficits. Any excess money of that month was set aside in a secret stash that only both of them knew. Since they were thick as thieves, this stash was later used to secretly buy home appliances, gadgets etc. to make their work easier.

There are many more such experiences and priceless lessons that I have learnt from my Wonder Woman. I have recognised the importance of some, and I am yet to learn the value of a few others. Today when I think back to all the times that I spent in her company; I regret my attitude. I could have spent more time learning from her, instead of complaining about getting bored. I feel ashamed. I regret all those missed opportunities, but also treasure all the wisdom she has shared with me. She believed in independence and free thought, she guards her freedom very fiercely to this day. She is still with us and alive, but due to her advanced age, she suffers from failing health and memory loss. All her valuable lessons and experiences are getting lost in the pages of time. The most amazing part of the story is that she still insists on doing her work independently and refuses to depend on others' help. She might not remember the life she lived, but her attitude is strongly ingrained and unchanged. There are yet some more lessons for me to observe and learn from her. Her fearlessness and courage to face hurdles with a straight spine are commendable. She may not tell me stories anymore, but her life and her journey is one big lesson that we can all learn from.

14

The Game Of Illusions

by Mansi Gupta

Aarya had turned 12, a day prior. She was, as usual, celebrating this day with her Naani (Maternal Grandmother) in the foothills of Shimla. Her birthday was a time when the family would plan their annual holiday to this perfectly cold, small town where fresh air was abundant, and the network connection was scarce. Just what the family needed to unwind.

Aarya would wait the entire year for this reunion, almost an extended slumber party with her most trusted companion! She could speak her mind to Naani, share her darkest secrets and yet feel that unconditional acceptance in Naani's warm hugs. Her grandmother had been her confidante since her childhood. Aarya could never forget when she confessed to Naani about the barbie doll incident when she was 7. Naani's reaction was indeed priceless!

Nishta, Aarya's classmate and childhood nemesis, had bought a new doll. It was so much better than every doll that Aarya had ever owned. Nishta's constant boasting about the features of the doll didn't help Aarya's growing jealousy. When no one was watching, Aarya pulled hard on the doll's legs. The massacre was gruesome for all the 7-year-old who had gathered for the playdate. Everyone knew who had done this. However, Nishta's mother had said, "If there isn't evidence, there's no one to blame!"

A month later, Aarya had confessed to Naani the gory details of the sad demise of the doll. Naani had instantly offered her a hug. She said, "Aaru, it must have been so hard for you to keep this as a secret. Something eating us up within must always be shared. If I am not around, you can trust your parents and if they ever yell at you, you come and tell me!"

Aarya was looking down with teary eyes, "But isn't this something, I should be punished for? Wouldn't they be right to yell?"

"Hmm. Well..." Naani kept the crochet threads aside, the sweater would have to wait for another day.

"Do you know why the Kauravas were 100 in the Indian Epic of Mahabharata and the Pandavas only 5?" she randomly asked with a pensive look on her face.

Puzzled Aarya moved her head from right to left indicating that no one had discussed this with her before.

"Well, my child. Kauravas are like our bad thoughts. They will always outnumber our good thoughts. We can't stop them from entering our mind. However, we can strengthen our Pandavas. The next time your evil thoughts take over, I am confident that you will understand that the Kauravas are getting stronger, we need to nurture them less. Not every thought needs to be acted upon! Jealousy, just like all other human emotions, is just an emotion. If you act upon it, you will give it power. If you don't, well, then the emotion will subside." Naani was now holding her little Aarya in her arms.

"Naaniiii. I think I want to gift Nishta the same doll again.

You think Mumma will allow me to break my piggy bank?" asked a guilt-laden Aarya.

Naani was smiling. She knew all her stories have a special place in the hearts of her grandchildren. More often than not, parents expect children to be fair, just and morally correct. Naani had made those mistakes with her children. She was now more accepting of flaws and incompetence. She couldn't look at people with disappointing eyes. Largely because, she believed, that expectations can ruin the core of relationships. Maybe that's why all her grandchildren trusted her with their darkest secrets. Especially Aarya.

Today on her 12th birthday and the first day of her periods, she needed no one other than Naani's aura around her. Aarya was now "healthy" a term that her family used often to substitute "fat." They didn't want to hurt her pre-teen, fragile, and quite aggressive, state of mind. These days, she would take seconds to burst into tears and wouldn't stop crying for hours at a stretch. Her father would get very upset about this behaviour. He would often blame the freedom, kids these days have, in terms of their online exposure. He wanted Aarya to undergo counselling. He felt that kids of her age group know much more than they can perceive. Her mother often dismissed all of this as "hormones"; but her grandmother always knew that she wanted someone to talk to her.

Someone to squeeze her for a long, long time and then say, "Let's go find that softy you like. Ice cream makes everything better."

Naani's room always had this very inviting odour. Lavender oil and rose water the two most prominent odours in the air of her room. She had a tiny changing area, near the bathroom, that had plenty of space for privacy. It had a huge mirror with beautiful light bulbs for the company to anyone who wanted some 'me' time. Aarya loved this space and would spend hours there, playing "Pretend" since she was a baby.

Naani would often play a game with Aarya which she named "The Game of Illusions." This was their well-kept secret and by far the best game Aarya enjoyed since she was a child.

"Enough Naani. I am 12 now! You need to tell me how this happens. I love this 'Game of Illusions' but I have to know how it works!" complained Aarya.

"Well. I ask you what you want to be? Your answer in one word- Happy, Confident, Smart. Then you go to my magic mirror and spend 15 minutes in those blue lights. You come back and tell me if you saw yourself in the mirror looking happy, confident, smart!

Yes or No!" said Naani in a pretty matter of fact manner.

"I know how to play the game Naani! My question is – How?! How is it that I always see myself Happy, confident, or whatever in your mirror but it doesn't work on mine?! My face has a smile, even my shoulders look straight like I am confident. Please, don't even try to tell me that's cause your 'mirror has magic.' I am 12 Naani not stupid." Aarya was irritated now.

Just like always, Granny smiled and said, "I promise, you will figure when you are older. Until then, believe in magic, my child."

"Ufffff," Aarya stomped, and she was out of Naani's room.

16 years had passed.

Aarya was visiting Shimla after so many years. She was

now, a mother of a beautiful baby girl. Aarya's mom had insisted that she drop the mithai (Indian sweets) at her maternal uncle's place.

It was the first time she was going there since Naani passed away. Naani had lived her life exactly how she wanted. Maybe, that is why, she passed away calmly, in her sleep. Not many ailments, just old age, perhaps. Aarya had not dared to talk about her loss to anyone.

She entered the house and could instantly smell the lavender oil. She hugged her uncle and asked, "Naani left her oils intact is it?"

Her uncle smiled and pointed at the incense sticks that were adorning the corners of the house. "Your Naani believed that mind was to be nurtured more than the body."

"Come, sit!" He gestured taking the baby from her hand.

"She often complained that our education system doesn't treat the mind very well. The mind is capable of unbelievable magic and hence our daily meditation is what we need," he was pointing at the incense sticks and smiling unknowingly.

"My mother was a mysterious woman. Beautiful, intellectual, mysterious woman!" said Uncle.

It was evident to Aarya that uncle missed Naani terribly. Some people leave the world, but their aura just sticks around. That positive sweet memory in the air when you talk about them. That twinkle in the eyes, the feel of sweet nostalgia!

After a few moments of both of them being quite out of words, Uncle cleared his throat and said, "Would you like to go to her room? She would always say that Aarya will come back to this mirror. I am sure you want to check it out."

Aarya jumped, almost forgetting her age

Uncle interrupted, "Don't forget the rules! Remember to first tell the mirror what you want to be!"

"Oh! Come on uncle. I cannot believe she told you about it. Did you guys do it too? Do you believe in this illusion?"

Uncle smiled and said, "Very much!"

Aarya rolled her eyes and said, "Uffff!"

Her daughter looked at her delighted as she ran up the stairs to check the mirror. She could almost hear her heartbeat with all the nervousness and anxiety.

Aarya was now stepping into Naani's room. Her eyes instantly landed on the sweater her Grandmother had knitted years ago. Her uncle had neatly wrapped it with a blue satin ribbon perhaps for her daughter. She remembered wearing it every year when she was in Shimla. The room still had that reassuring aura, her plants were blooming even after her. So much had changed, yet so much remained the same. She walked slowly to the corner where the mirror sat, welcoming anyone who wanted a peak of their reflection. She shut the door and sat there looking deeply into the eyes that looked back at her. She couldn't remember how much time had passed.

She stepped out, teary-eyed. She could feel a weight on her chest, a lump in her throat, as if her emotions no longer knew their boundaries. They were looking to see the outer world and they kept flowing, in the form of tears.

"How? How is this still happening? Please, uncle. Tell me. How do I look so happy in her mirror?"

Uncle smiled and said, "Reflections my child! Reflections are not what we are. Reflections are what we believe we are. If you believe you are happy or beautiful, you will reflect that in every mirror and every person you meet. If you believe you are successful, every eye will reflect it. Illusions are not magical. Belief is!

Naani believed in you and she was your safe space, hence her mirror was a mystery! Make the world your safe space, my child. Go witness the magic!" Uncle sounded so much like Aarya's long lost companion. Her lips were shivering, and she could feel the tingling down her spine almost as if Naani's presence could be felt around.

Aarya touched the mirror with teary eyes. She could feel her Naani's squishy hugs. She thought of the million times that she had stared into her mirror back at home, wondering why her diet wasn't working. Why was the pimple the most evident spot on her face? Why the dark circles? Was she reflecting all this, all along?

So much we create, unknowingly!

15

The Enchantress

by Debjyoti Das

As the pale misty white light of winter dawn was breaking, I felt the urge of having a cup of hot tea after taking a long walk, fascinated by the exquisite beauty of the early morning. I abruptly stopped before a wayside tea stall. It was then I spotted her.

She was in her late teens, clad in a long Kurti, scars of overuse and dart. Confidently she came and stood before me. Her luscious lips parted; a mysterious smile flooded her full-face. Instantly I felt a familiarity to her.

Her restless but comprehensible stare compelled me to offer her a cup of hot tea. Willingly she accepted and relished the hot liquid taking small sips and looking at me with her dreamy eyes. Sipping the last drop, her lips parted again for a complimentary smile. Without uttering a word, she walked away sensuously.

I realised it was not my first meeting with her. Although it seemed an ethereal encounter, I could recall that I had noticed her earlier during my school days while walking through the lanes of Ballygunge. A teenage girl, she was walking hurriedly, a suave expression on her face. Sometimes I had found her strolling in a sombre mood. Whenever I noticed her, I always felt that same sense of belonging to her.

"Excuse me, would you like to join us?"

The female voice compelled me to look up at her. A lady in her early twenties was standing before my table as I was browsing through the pages of a literary magazine bought from a stall before entering the Coffee House. The same familiar face with a mysterious smile, looking straight at me. Her profound eyes as serene as morning dew, expressing intriguing yet innocent desire to talk with me. Perhaps the literary magazine in my hand attracted her attention to approach me to join with her group of friends. I hesitated for a moment then obliged like an obeyed child.

"Let me introduce you to my friends," she said. The warmth of her voice brought back my comfort level. One by one she introduced all her friends. The discussion went on for long, from literature to politics. Cups of black coffee, favourite among the regulars of the College Street Coffee House, only fuelled our conversations. A university student like her had vast knowledge in different subjects, which was enough to feel attracted to a sapiosexual like me. She had given a good company to me during the animated discussions, asking my opinions. Her friends called her Tilottama, an alluring name as seducing as her beauty, divinely created, one who is composed of the finest and highest qualities no doubt, I thought.

It turned out to be a memorable evening for me. But to my dismay, she left suddenly having some pending works to be completed. I hadn't got the opportunity to take her contact details, which was awkward to ask for, especially in the first meeting among her friends.

Three months later I was loitering around the wayside stalls at Kalighat temple road, that led to the famous temple of Goddess Kali in Kolkata. The stalls had beautiful miniature idols of Gods and Goddesses, created by the skilled craftsmen. I stopped to admire the artistic beauty of those idols. Suddenly a lady came and stood beside me and instructed the shopkeeper in a gentle voice to hand over something that she wanted to examine closely.

The voice made me alert, for it was the same special voice that my ears were already familiar with. There she stood, elegantly in a yellow saree, the traditional attire of a Bengali lady. Demure yet confident. A great sense of dignity reflected in her behaviour. Mesmerized, I was looking straight at her like an idiot, watching her intently. She glanced at me, the same mysterious smile on her parted lips. After some bargain she bought the article and walked away elegantly, giving a parting glance at me.

"Do you know her, sir?"

The interrogation of the shopkeeper helped me to get back to my senses.

"Yes… No, I don't think I'm known to her." I replied. Paying the money, I left the shop hurriedly. The shopkeeper kept on staring at me with a mocking grin in his face.

Her traditional look remained fresh in my mind for a protracted period. Whenever I stepped out, I searched her among the vast multitude, unknowingly, as if a habit that might be defined as a lecherous gaze. Even I mistook others, thinking it was she, but found a mere look alike. I started comparing her with others but in vain. For she had incomparable beauty, matchless grace, an angel whom a man would idolize her to be a perfect life partner forever.

The whole city turned into a glowing furnace of the summer heat, longing to get relief. The day was humid, indicating afternoon rain. As the sun completed half of its diurnal journey, the enormous black clouds gradually made themselves ready to plunge the city to darkness to shower its bounty in the form of torrential rain. It seemed the whole city was eagerly awaiting the cold relief. A soothing cold breeze was already giving the message of its arrival.

Walking on a long stretch of footpath, I felt a comforting effect of the cold breeze. Big raindrops started to fall soon. A fragrance hit my nostrils, petrichor, the parched earth was calming down releasing the heat in the form of an intoxicating aroma from the nearby Central Park.

I didn't feel running away or taking shelter from the incoming rain. I had already made up my mind to get myself thoroughly drenched, an exhilarating feeling of taking a shower in the maiden rain of the monsoon in the heart of my favourite city. The city that could change its character suddenly, non-inertia, a concoction, from traditional to contemporary, natural touch of tenderness over the vast glory of fashionable artificiality.

A big banyan tree standing proudly by the roadside, surrounding the high-rises, proclaiming its age-old glory by its extending branches, giving shadowy shelter to man and the aerial lives. I accepted the privilege to enjoy the monsoon shower standing under it. But not alone, as she was already there, with an open umbrella holding over her head. Tilottama, her enticing stare drew me near to her.

"Hello, you can share my umbrella," she said, extending her arm that held the umbrella. I stood so near to her, that I sensed the smell of her body, mixed with artificial perfume. I felt dizzy by the intoxicating aroma of her body with the rain-soaked earth, taking a deep breath, wading through a dream-like state. I couldn't recall our conversation, but I could remember her smiling face. She laughed like an ever-flowing river, Kallolini, as she would be described. The incessant monsoon shower portrayed the image of a skilled danseuse flowing with gaiety, Tilottama transformed to Kallolini, displaying her feminine strength of fertility and progress.

Ever since these encounters, she was never out of my sight or mind. I saw her on Howrah Bridge, at the lawn of Victoria Memorial, inside the Indian Museum or National Library, under Shahid Minar, illusively sometimes fair or dark-complexioned in her full bloom, putting on either gorgeous saree or poorly clad, exposing her physical charms with restlessness in her large eyes. She was ever-present for me in the lanes and by-lanes, on a crowded metro platform, inside a bright colourful shopping mall, multiplex or nightclub, sometimes formal or informal outfits, either impassive or sometimes lively and elegant, jiving madly in a white top and mini skirt exposing her smooth voluptuous exciting shins.

The bountiful monsoon gave way to charming autumn, the city transformed herself to a beautiful maiden worshipping the feminine strength in the form of Goddess Durga. It was a pleasant time for me to get her glimpse everywhere. In every street throughout the city I roamed the whole day and night to see her, the charming beauty like a Urvashi, Tilottama or like an ever-flowing river Ganga, Kallolini. The week-long carnival always turned out for me to be the best days of the year.

I don't know who she was, might be surreal, but I can now understand that she is my love, whom I adore, an idol of my romance. True, that I have possessed her in my heart. It might be she transcended herself to allure me with her animated alacrity. I could not deny my acquaintance with her. It might be she was delineated as Tilottama or Kallolini but if I had the power of a wizard, I would fascinate her as eternal Urvashi or Umrao Jan, in reality. The enchanting power of her always drew me near to her and felt homesick whenever I went abroad. She is still a mixture of dream and reality to me. She is none but my dearest darling KOLKATA, my city whom I adore and love.

16

A Thank You Note

by Elizabeth Caroline Palaparthi

Dear Mom and Dad,

This is an appreciation post for you guys.

First off, I'm grateful to both of you. I can't thank you enough for everything you guys have done for me. I love both of you immensely from the bottom of my heart. But I guess I'd like to give a little extra love to dad because mom, you already have enough love from everyone else.

You don't need extra love. Just kidding haha, I love both of you equally. Okay so let's begin this roller coaster ride with mom.

Thank you, mom, for bringing me into this world, for all the efforts you have made to make me into what I am today. I love you and I'm grateful for the way you brought me up. Even if I was ever given a chance, I wouldn't change a single thing about my past. I'm happy about the way me and Saroj (my younger brother) are raised.

From the beginning I know I wasn't an easy child as I am very picky and particular about everything. Starting from clothes to food, I am extremely choosy. But you've always allowed me to be myself and never forced me to do things that I don't like.

You've been hard on me about stuff related to my education and I thank you very much for that. It brought me to where I am today. You've not just helped me in my studies, but also made sure that I was a part of various other things like sports and cultural activities. I know how difficult it was for you to shift towns and manage to work as well as looking after a fussy baby. I appreciate the efforts you've put in to raise me.

During my early years of schooling, I found it exceedingly difficult to cope up with the smallest changes. Every little thing like changing bench partners or sections used to give me a really hard time making friends. Even today, I don't really like change. But you've taught me how to get over it and taught me that changes are important in one's life and by welcoming change, I am welcoming new experiences. Thank you for always helping me and Babloo with our school projects.

One such example is during my schooling; you were the whole reason for me to switch schools after my 7th grade. I was so reluctant to go to a new school because I was worried that I would not find friends in this whole new environment. But you made me understand that it's okay to feel so and with time I'll adjust to everything and learn to enjoy it. Like always, your words turned out to be true. Not only did I make good friends, but I was also chosen to be a part of the school cabinet. It is a part of my life that I will cherish forever and I'm happy that you pushed me into it.

Next came Inter which was truly a roller coaster ride for me. You've seen me be in the toughest part of my life till today and I wouldn't have been able to go through it without your help.

Thank you for accompanying me to Pune for my Swimming nationals. I still remember how you woke me up early at 5 am and helped me jump into the ice-cold water for practice. And later during the day when it was time for my 100 mts freestyle event, you were there all along cheering for me. You are the perfect company anyone could ask for. After my events were done, we went around that place and went to meet one of our relatives who was living very far away from the stadium. I remember you letting me buy a new swimming costume there which is one of my all-time favourites, I still have that costume with me till today. Hopefully, I'll find some time to start swimming again. Miss those days so much.

Now let's talk about the fun part.

I love how we share the same interests, how we love to shop and buy junk and it's amazing how energetic and enthusiastic you are even at the end of the day after all your work at the hospital. Even though you are a very busy radiologist with a lot of responsibilities on your shoulders, you always find time to spend with us and make us a happy family. You usually never say no to any of my wishes. You are very open-minded and chill with a lot of things. It makes me want to share everything in my life with you, without the fear of being judged.

You are generous and caring. No matter who it is, you always care for them as if they're one of your own. You've given me some great values which I'll remember throughout my life.

Thank you for always pushing me to take that extra mile in everything that I do.

You're always my go-to person for everything, be it

academics or sports or about general life. I know that you will always be just a phone call away. I don't know if I can live up to your expectations, but I hope I'll make you proud someday.

Now it's about the silent and a little more sophisticated parent, my dad.

I love you for the way you are. Don't change a bit for anyone in this world, I know you wouldn't but just saying haha. So basically, I've grown up being a little scared of you. I don't exactly know the reason but I'm glad that I'm over it now. I'm sure you know this by now.

I remember how you would help me with my struggle to learn Telugu. According to you even today my Telugu is not good. I don't think I'm that bad and I can live with it.

I love how you make our Education your priority. You've always taught us to pursue our goals no matter what obstacles come along. You've spent all your time looking out for us. From helping Babloo excel in his table tennis competitions to helping me with my studies, we've come a long way.

You are the world's best and my favourite teacher. And I'm sure Babloo would agree with this too because I know how he loves to have you by his side to guide him while he's playing his table tennis matches.

Thank you for always being so supportive of me during my childhood. Picking me up and dropping me to my swimming classes every day wasn't an easy task.

Thank you for playing a major role in helping me get through Inter. Mom was always there but if it weren't for you, I wouldn't be doing MBBS right now.

You are my inspiration to be a surgeon and I hope and pray that I will become a plastic surgeon like you one day. I know that I am very impatient as a person. I hope I learn to develop some patience like you as your level of patience is remarkable.

Now that I am doing medicine, I understand the amount of uncertainty that comes with it. I have huge respect for what you have become in life.

It surprises me as to how the worldly things don't fascinate you so much, you are always more focused on the non-materialistic things in life, and that is great quality.

You've encouraged us to develop a sense of individuality.

Thank you for changing your lifestyle to help us get through ours. I'm sure that the relentless efforts that you've put in to shape us into better individuals will pay off someday.

Thank you for telling me what I am capable of. For giving me the support that I need to build a dream to chase after. And for believing me that I have the talent to accomplish my goals. Thank you for your love of sports which has raised two sportspersons: me and my brother.

I appreciate how you mention something once and make sure that you never bug us with constant reminders even though I love it when mom does it. You've helped me realize that anything is possible with hard work and dedication. I wouldn't have learnt it any other way. I hope that I'll make you proud one day.

You guys have been my pillars of strength no matter what and I know you will continue to be so. Both of you have been raised by a single parent and have reached this stage of life after going through a lot of hardships. You are so good at parenting in your ways that I couldn't have asked for better. Without each of you, I'd be nowhere near the person I am and the person I am still working on becoming. There aren't enough words in the world to express my appreciation, but I think this is a good start. I owe you one (many).

Hope I've brought a smile on your face while reading this. I love both of you so much.

Elizabeth Caroline

17

My Companero

by Praneetha Sivalenka

Have you ever wondered why girls are often referred to as "Daddy's Princess"? Or have you ever heard a mother complaining to her neighbour that her daughter is pampered a lot by the daughter's dad, who never allows his wife to shout at his baby princess?

Most of your answers would be YES!

Here is my story of one such dad who will be further referred to as "Nanna Garu."

"My Nanna Garu is the best." Of course! Which daughter would like to start her story without quoting this line? Here we go...

Mr. Krishna Rao is my nanna Garu. He was born & brought up in a joint family. He started his part-time jobs right from the age of 17. He always worked hard and ensured that he never stayed at home sitting idle. At the age of 34, he got married to Dr. Bhavani. We're three siblings. Me, my elder brother and my twin brother. Ours is a happy going family with a lot of silly fights. My Nanna Garu is calm & patient. He's an amazing singer and he's an avid reader. He likes to be bossy, but he often fails because whenever he tries to order us to do something, we make him smile! He helps all of us a lot. If he ever went out to stay at our relative's place, then our whole day would get messed up because no one in our family can organize things in the way he does. He likes perfection.

Till the age of 10, I was often scared of Nanna Garu. Maybe that's how I showed my respect towards him. I used to quickly cover myself with the blanket and pretended to sleep as soon as I heard Nanna's footsteps, which used to give a signal that he's home. I often gulped down the big glass of milk & stood in front of dad after which he used to help me get ready for my school. To be more precise, he ironed my uniform, helped me tie my school tie, kept my lunch and filled my water bottle. After which he had to redo this whole set of things for both of my siblings too. He held our bags and walked along with us till we got an auto-rickshaw. While returning home, after dropping us to the school, he never took an auto. He always walked back home just to save that money for the next day's auto fare. He could have asked an auto driver to pick us up every day and drop all three of us at the school. But neither he nor my mom preferred it. Both of them wanted to ensure us that we were always in the safest hands and to be more precise in their hands!

Later we shifted our home, from where my school was of walkable distance. Even then Nanna Garu accompanied three of us to reach the school every day. Those were one of the best days of my life. There used to be a general store before we entered my school lane where dad bought chocolates for us almost every single day. It felt as if we were the only kids on the earth who get to eat chocolates every day. It could be the last week of the month or first week of the month, buying chocolates for us became mandatory. He never denied buying for us even if it was an empty pocket day. Maybe this is how true love is, it makes you do everything even if you have nothing.

When I was in 6th grade, we had a chapter which consisted of topics on adolescence. When my science teacher told me that that was the age where attraction & infatuation usually come into play, I was wondering how someone will ever have that short-lived passion or admiration towards someone alien to them. I haven't known what love is while a lot of my friends fell in their first love already! As I grew up, though I had an amazing & exuberant childhood, I never knew what this four-letter word meant because I have never used it or heard someone from my family using it. Neither I fell in love nor did I encourage my friends' love. A lot of thoughts ran through my mind. I was passionate about knowing the secrets of love.

I didn't know the answers to a lot of things. Then came a day where my teacher asked my whole class to write an essay on the topic, 'My Parents'. At the end of the essay, she asked us to mention ONE thing which we wanted our parents to do that they've never done. I wrote everything that struck my mind. I knew how mom & dad worked hard to get both the ends to meet. Never was a day where mom & dad went out alone. Neither they attended kitty parties, nor did they go for movies. Both of them sacrificed their happiness for us and filled joy in our lives. That's how my free birds who dreamt of flying high in the sky were then happy to fly down for the family they love. I finished my whole essay within just fifteen minutes.

When I was about to submit, I realized that I haven't mentioned that one thing my teacher asked me to mention. I thought till the last minute and couldn't find any single thing that my parents didn't do for me. That is the moment I realized what my parents were. That day I might have lost marks for not answering the teacher's question, but I've received immense satisfaction which cannot be evaluated with so-called grades. I repeat there was not even one single thing that I could think of about what mom & dad have not given me.

That's how I finally realized that love has been embedded in the person who woke me up and woke himself up for me, worked hard for me and did everything to make sure I have had my necessities done. That's when I knew love is not a single word it's zillion dreams, million responsibilities and a universe of understanding. Maybe love originates from parents and not from God because God wouldn't have been God if he didn't receive his share of love from his parents.

Just like the saying goes 'little things matter', in each step of our lives, dad ensured that every little thing was taken care of in the best of his ability. We received everything at the right time and in the right way. And that's what makes me feel proud of the dad I've. When it came to visit my grandmother, if it was only him who wanted to go, then he always went by bus. But when all three of us (me & my siblings) were also asked to come then he never took us by bus. We were always offered a comfortable journey.

While the majority of my friends' parents pushed them for tuitions our parents encouraged us to play outside. That paved a way for my elder brother to step into professional cricket. We had the freedom to study whenever we wanted. It was completely okay even if we skipped studying for a whole week because we were taught, by our parents, to grasp the information and not to mug up sentences. That's how I enjoyed studying. The only thing I was forced to do was to watch old movies of N.T.R Garu and A.N.R Garu because they were my dad's favourite heroes. However, I loved watching those movies with my dad beside me.

Until my 9th grade, everything was smooth at home. When I stepped to 10th me & my twin brother realized that the school in which we were studying wouldn't help us out to acquire complete knowledge of the syllabus prescribed. That school had limited faculty. And there was no one to teach physics and math. We, however, managed our first two months with the help of YouTube videos.

Elder brother noticed it and took this issue to our parents. They always considered every issue that was related to our education in the best way possible. They left no stone unturned when it came to helping us find the best school. In that process, paying high fee for our institutions became mandatory. The costs were inevitable, but dad never hesitated to take loans to offer us the best education and to support mom. They always shared their expenses and their efforts in bringing us up were immense. Nanna Garu knew he was scraping the barrel, but he had no other option. Then, Nanna Garu considered only two things. One was to ensure us our future and the other was to ensure mom that she was not alone.

After I and my twin passed our 10th grade we were left free to choose our career while our relatives forced Nanna Garu to join us in the M.P.C stream because they wanted to see us settled as Engineers. But dad never took decisions on our behalf. He asked us if we were okay with the plan. We denied and he respected our decision. That's how easy it was for us to be completely open with our decisions. Love is not always offering the best things for your loved ones; sometimes it is accepting their normal requests & allowing them to fly. This is one of the most amazing concepts of love that I have learned from dad.

Almost a year ago we heard the good news, but It said that mom had to go out of town for one year to render her services as a principal in one of the welfare colleges. That seemed like a solution for all our financial problems but none of us was truly ready to stay at home without her. Mom was worried too. That's when Nanna Garu assured mom that he'd manage all the household chores & would cook for us every day. Hence for me, True love is always above the romantic phase because anyone can be romantic with you, but everyone cannot take up responsibilities for you. Everyone can say 'I love you' but everyone cannot be your 'loved one'. Only when you know that a person is something beyond being romantic that's when you find your perfect pair. And if that person is found to have a majority of the qualities that your dad possesses it's like an added feather to your hat.

In a country where women are often restricted to stay indoors and limit their dreams, dad offered his hand to help her achieve everything she wanted to. Mom was never forced to change her surname. He ensured all the hurdles are taken off the way. He's broad-minded and always tries to understand mom's mood swings which arise due to various external pressures. Respecting people irrespective of their gender, caste & creed is dad's thing and that's one of my most favourite features in him.

As mom left for her designated place it was now dad's turn to learn different things to satisfy us. My dad and I shared our household work. We took turns and cooked. If I cooked for lunch, he cooked for dinner. If I was ever busy with my assignments, he never reminded me to work. Instead, he did my share of work too. Whenever I was on my period, he took utmost care of mine, cooked the food I liked and never allowed me to work. Those were the days when I and Nanna became a lot close to each other. Dad took a lot of stress to clear the debts but soon he realized that we're going to kick back to normal and the things are going to be okay.

He dedicated himself to every work he did for us. He also offered his helping hand to his friends and colleagues when they were in financial problems. He often stood for them even if it was difficult for him to provide that aid. He also used his credit cards for this purpose. He used to deal with everything with a lot of patience. I observed everything keenly right from childhood and that's when I learned the tricks to be patient and subtle. I tackled every tough situation with these two tools that I've gained from my dear dad. I and dad share the best relationship. Whenever he shouts at me, I just stare at him with a smile on my face. That's when he comes back to me and conveys the same thing in a soft tone again. Now he screams at me only to get that smile on my face. Dad shared all his secrets with me. Whenever he's low, it was only me who knew the reason. I became his best friend that way. It's been six months now that dad stopped sipping his favourite drink for all of us.

Yes, dads are superheroes. They can learn anything and leave everything for the family they love.

Dad allows me to wear everything I'm comfortable in. Whenever I cry it is the dad who enters my room and consoles me. He makes me laugh. He shares everything with me. He allows me to go everywhere including night outs. When it comes to going out for parties, everyone at home denies. Then my super dad enters the conversation and convinces all those who oppose me. He gives me a positive spirit of freedom.

Three months passed in this lockdown and I've had the best days of my life with dad.

That bond which I always wanted with my Nanna Garu is forever present now. We binge watch episodes of Ramayana and Mahabharata together. We talk about celebrities, politics, movies, sports, and a lot more things. Nanna Garu also got habituated with the word 'bro' now. So, we started calling each other "bro". From being scared to call him up loud to scaring him up with my loud voice, from being less talkative to being over-talkative, from resting in different rooms to sleeping next to each other, from complaining about mom's food to cooking together, every single thing that happened this year will be cherished for life. His sacrifices are immeasurable. His dedication is deep. His love has no bounds. He is my dad and I'm proud of that fact. Because everything fades, his love doesn't.

I hurt you never,

I love you forever,

Hey dear father,

This is your hardcore lover.

18

It All Started With A Crayon

by Adyasha Pattnaik

I was six years old when my dad had a transfer and we had to move to Hyderabad. A week after shifting, I had my admission done in a school which was nearby to the locality we had moved into. Joining a new school was exhausting because I was sheepish and introverted.

My parents had bought me a grey-coloured Spiderman school bag, a Pokemon water bottle, and a shiny red pencil box, all of which would twinkle any six-year old's eyes, and neither of which seemed appealing nor delightful to me. My eyes didn't twinkle, I was having a nervous breakdown instead. I never entertained change 'cause it was tiring and I was extremely bad at it.

The first day of primary school is till date one of the hardest days I had ever had to pull off. As soon as I stepped inside the classroom, there were forty pairs of eyes gazing at me.

A drop of sweat slithered down my neck as I walked past each of them. Standing in front of a whole lot of people whom I was meeting for the first time and getting introduced to had my stomach in knots.

I noticed an empty bench with no human proximity fifty centimetres around it and raced there before our teacher could make me sit beside somebody. I sat down and the forty pairs of eyes were still glued on me until the teacher brought back their attention to her.

I had spent the entire day pretty much by myself. A bunch of six-year-old girls had passed by me whispering and giggling during breaks. The day was starting to get tiring, and I was more than happy about the fact that it was the last period of the day.

It was art class, and we were learning how to draw and colour an orange. I took out my drawing book and started to draw. A while later, a boy turned around asking if I had an orange crayon. This was my only chance to make a conversation with an actual person but, he simply took the crayon and turned away. I had to wait the entire time until he had finished colouring.

While I watched everybody getting their drawing books signed, my waiting hours for getting my crayon back had turned into an eternity. Although, asking him to give it back had occurred to me but it seemed like a herculean task. So, I sat there doing nothing about it at all.

I finally stacked up every last ounce of my courage and asked the boy, "I had given you my orange crayon. Where is it?"

He turned around and said, "I had already given it to you" and turned away again.

As much as I did enjoy our chat, the fact that I had lost a crayon and I had wasted more than half of the class sitting idly waiting for him to return it, made me panic. Searching for it didn't help anymore because the class had ended. While leaving the class, our teacher said he would check the others next week, which did not make me feel any better.

To sum up my day,

I had lost a crayon on the first day of school, made no friends and the only person I had spoken to, was a boy who was responsible for losing it. It was the worst first day of school any six-year-old could ever have.

I had searched everywhere for my crayon but had no luck in finding it. Apart from being an introvert, I was sensitive and the first thing I did after I gave up was cry.

The entire class seemed to have left except for one girl. She came over to me, kneeled, and asked why was I crying, I told her that I lost my orange crayon and couldn't get my drawing book signed either. She sat beside me, pulled out a box of crayons, and handed me an orange one from it.

"Hi. My name is Sparsha," she smiled offering me a handshake. She was the only person who spoke to me that day without any selfish intentions and the only person who wanted to be my friend. I acknowledged her handshake with wet hands 'cause of all the tears. She even helped me pack my bag and walked with me to the front gate of the school.

Back then I didn't know that an orange crayon would serve as a steppingstone for a friendship that I would cherish for a lifetime to come.

***

Constant bullying and mocking for hitting puberty too soon and being oversensitive were how the rest of the ten years of my schooling went. And throughout the entire time, Sparsha was there to comfort me, defend me and protect me. She was always there when I needed her.

Around halfway through my tenth, I was made aware of all the objectifying and sickening comments being passed on about me by my classmates. In a matter of a few days, all of the secrets were out in the open. During every break, there were a series of arguments that would go on between me and my classmates.

The ugliness of the fights had started turning into revenge plots. Sparsha and I were shuffled after class four and met only during breaks and free class hours and now even that seemed to be impossible. They neither would let her in nor let me out. They had a fight or two with Sparsha when she would try to come inside to meet me.

They had proved to have annoyed every single bone in my body and I had to let myself out of the class. But it wasn't easy. They neither touched me, nor did they block my way anymore, but passing one vile comment on me did the job of making me stay back and also trigger a meltdown.

Sparsha had somehow managed to get into my class, saw me having one of my worst meltdowns, and just sat there holding me.

"I know all of this is harsher than ever but you gotta be strong because you know you are not any of those things," she said.

Our section had a free hour after break and Sparsha did not. Yet she stayed with me missing her period and made sure I was completely alright.

Much later after the incident happened, she told me that the day she had barged into my class, my classmates had told her an awful lot of filth right on her face while she sat there comforting me. She had broken down later that day too and never told me because she wanted to be strong for me.

Taking harder blows than me to make sure I was alright is why I loved her the most.

Being the most rock-solid support system throughout my bad times just kept increasing her value in my life more and more. We were inseparable.

***

Class nine was the year of the disaster whose secret hasn't been out yet. One major thing that Sparsha and I loved doing was hang out in the girl's washroom. In my defence, it was quite clean and not many used it for the loo. There was a sanitary pad vending machine that we had finally managed to break open and smuggle most of the pads away. We did it every time they fixed that and never got suspected.

On one of many smuggling days, we decided on doing something even wilder and we had our other friends hanging with us that day too. The washroom was huge, empty, and clean so we thought of holding a race. For the wild part, we were supposed to race with carrying somebody on our back. The race began and I was on Sparsha's back. We won, and the excitement led to me falling with a "crack" whose sound echoed in the washroom. She hadn't realized that she had thrown me down and the pain hit me thirty seconds after the fall.

I was rushed to the emergency room and my mother arrived shortly after. In the evening I went for an X-ray and found out I had a nasty broken collar bone that probably needed surgery.

My parents hadn't asked me how I fell, yet. After we visited the doctor, they sat me down and asked me about it. I had to keep Sparsha totally in the clear and had a story made up already. I told them that the washrooms weren't clean, and they never wiped off the excess water. The floors were slippery, and the water reduced more of the floor's friction.

My parents were furious and went over to the school the next day with tons of complaints. Our principal had to take in more than ever that day. Cleanliness of not just that one washroom but every other washroom of the school was all that was taken care of for the next two months.

A day after my accident, Sparsha had come over to meet me and once our moms got busy with talking and we were left alone in my room, she started crying. Her meltdown was pretty bad, and she was filled with immense amounts of guilt after seeing the condition I was in.

She had apologized for it a thousand times. I told her that no matter what I would always have her back and it was all an accident and that it was never her fault and telling all of this to her somehow made her wail even louder. She had stayed for an hour and her crying just wouldn't stop.

After a month of rest, I was back to school for my exams. After my mom dropped me off in front of the gate, Sparsha was always there to carry my bag to the library where I was supposed to be writing my exams and help me carry it back after they were done. I had my shoulder braces on for almost three months and she had taken care of every little need of mine the entire time.

Having her around me all the time helped me cope with the pain in a much better way. The thought of losing a friend like her was far from being unimaginable.

***

The intermediate academic year was a huge turning point in our friendship. She had moved to another place in the same city, and she had gotten into a school of her choice which was close to the place where she stayed. However, I had decided to do it from the same school I did my tenth from.

The school wasn't the same without her. The fact that she was aware of every little detail of my life from the time we met made me lonely. I had developed a lot of trust issues with people now and I was dependent on her. Blabbing anything and everything to her helped me weigh down my stress a notch. Now that she was away, I thought I would go back to being lonely again.

We texted almost every day when we started school. She was having a tough time making friends and I was having a tough time trying not to make any more friends. The only reason being my dislike for the people who belonged to that very same school. Besides, starting a conversation or making a friend had never been my cup of tea and Sparsha had played a major role in getting me out of my shell. I had already started to build a bubble around me again.

I did go on to make two incredible friends much later on but neither of them could take her place. I was extremely introverted and Sparsha had managed to bring me up to the level of an ambivert. She was as extroverted as anybody could ever get, even more so.

She did have starting problems at first but managed to make a truckload of friends later on and that bothered me. Insecurity was one of the many strong feelings that I had whenever she sent any pictures or spoke about any of her new friends. I was having a great time too, but a part of me always felt that I would eventually get replaced.

Pretending to like any of her friends and seeming happy for her had started to mentally exhaust me. One such day she was telling me about her friends, an argument broke, and tons of complaints and blames started to surface. It lasted for more than a week until we stopped talking anymore. Neither of us tried initiating a conversation for the next six months or so.

Two years ago, before the fight happened neither of us knew how difficult maintaining a friendship would be. The gap of six months was the time of growth for both of us.

Accepting that the two of us would be making more friends and meeting more people later on in our lives was a huge milestone.

Six months later, when the two of us were decked up to attend colleges and move on with our respective lives, we decided to meet for one last time before leaving. The two of us had taken every important step of our life together and college was the one that topped all the others.

The meet turned out to be surprisingly normal. We never talked about our fight and we had loads to catch up on and as the conversation continued, we realized there was nothing that had changed after all. We had a few stumbles, but we had found our way back to each other.

It's been sixteen years and we don't talk every day or text for that matter. Both of us have more friends than we had imagined we would ever have. But we know what place the two of us hold in each other's lives. And that is never changing.

***

Last year was not such a good year for her and she was into a lot of depression. Sparsha is among those who love and never expect anything back but this time it was different. She had given love, care, trust, and had built up expectations more than what was ever asked for. The result had left her with a broken heart, tons of trust issues, and all her love was drained out.

Every time she felt low during those times, I would write something about us and post it on social media with our picture and that would cheer her up instantly. Little things are what mattered the most to her. What I did to cheer her up couldn't even be compared to what she had been doing for me all along. After all these years, she didn't expect anything back except for thanking me to be by her side every time.

Sparsha is a person who dreams and works hard to fulfil each of them. Watching her grow stronger and stronger with time has made me respect her and our friendship even more.

It's been sixteen years since the day we met, and we have seen a lot together than individually combined. Our bond has gotten stronger, and we have grown to be better people because we always had each other at every step of our life. Relating to every single "BFF goal" in most of the TV series that I watch reminds of every beautiful memory of ours. Having a person impact your life so much that it scares you to ever watch them go away is beautiful and frightening at the same time. But growing past every single one of those times is what builds a stronger trust among two people.

You might have a best friend, but you can never have a Sparsha. She is the only one and I get to keep her for life.

***

It all started with a crayon and the end? Well, there isn't any.

19

10,356 Kms Of Destiny

by Bhavya Rao

It was a Sunday morning that she called me asking for the route to my place for the nth time, though this wasn't the first time she was visiting me alone. As classic Vanika, this was the utmost expected act of her. My mom enquired on what kind of meal would she prefer the normal or the complicated one because there's this one rule that whenever Vanika visits home there has to be something more than ordinary at home because that's how much she loves food more than anything and that's how much my mom loves Vanika more than me (best friends steal your moms).

I've known Vanika for three years now. I've been there when she lost her mom and hope for life and also when she was hiding those little hickeys saying wild insect bites. Though I've not known her for long we have shared enough affection for each other to last an eternity. So, this time when she visited me and teamed up with my mom while mocking me, she brought in something that was a very insignificant part of her life, which turned out to be very important and pivotal to mine. Later we asked Tisa to join for the meal and a little gossip. And that's where the very beginning to this tale emerged. We brought up the very interesting talk of mentioning Ashish once again who happens to be Vanika's ex-boyfriend about whom we've known very little. We've heard so much about him from Vanika and Anirudh, but we've known him very little, maybe Vanika too. So as usual I started mocking Vanika by trying to talk very high in the regard of Ashish and how appealing his appearance was, the kind nature he possessed, how magnificent he was as a man. Vanika showed no sign of being upset and came up with the "I know he's good" comeback which roasted us in return. Tiya had to mess around and with time. played a random card and asked if we could add him in our social media accounts and Vanika barely made any excuses or act of her being upset, which we presumed to be an agreeable answer. Though she warned us about a few things like how he'd get furious about a few issues and not to mention her name while conversing with him as that may bring in chances for chaos to occur. This wasn't something new or something we didn't expect from the situation. And after listening to so many precautions and warnings I wasn't looking for any interesting conversation and of course, I didn't expect him to start a conversation that early.

This is how my story took a start with Ashish, with a text message from him saying how the meme I shared was utmost relatable. Yeah, it was a pretty bland conversation starter which eventually turned to endless talks, stories roasts and knowing each other. Until that moment I've just heard about him in very occasional phases. But after that one day, he became a daily routine I was engrossed into. We started with basic mockery and roasts which ended in talks about life and dark secrets spilt out. It never felt like we've not known each other our whole life. Instead it always felt like we grew up together. That's how much we related to most of the topics we discussed.

Finally, that's how I found comfort in this stranger living miles apart from me. That's how our bond took the pace and continued my tale with Ashish, the only human that allowed me to talk for hours without checking the clock for once and also helped me learn to be insecure about nothing and made me feel no guilt while asking the most irrelevant questions that might have brought a look of me being not very intellectual and at the same time left me the opportunity to roast him about everything.

This man here made me learn the true essence of being magnificent, he was like that classic novel story which would be very slow and not understandable in the very beginning but with every chapter passing you'd just keep falling in love with the characters and then you find the whole literature, plot, literally every letter, little characteristics, the little scratches on the cover, those little curled edges of those old paled out pages and almost every single detail of the book to be the most beautiful thing you ever came across. He had answers to all of my questions. And for a spoiler alert, I've never met him in my whole life and yet he knows all about me right from what issues I've with different people to what days I might menstruate. Well, Ashish, is that kind of person whom you'd want to hate so much and yet couldn't keep yourself from falling in love with.

As audience might already assume, I am madly in love with this stranger I met in virtual life, let me say my love for him is platonically just like how you fall in love with something that inspires you in a very unusual and unexpected manner that you wouldn't stop talking about how magical the sight was. This is a similar one as this isn't a love story. This is just a tale of love and admiration between two grown-ups racing in their own pace with the moving world and without any knowledge, match with each other's pace and meet each other in very odd scenarios and bond despite staying seas apart.

It's been just 4 months we've been talking and yet there hasn't been a day that passes without each of us sending each other the perfect relatable memes, nostalgic music albums or song recommendations and of course video calls for roasting each other, although I get roasted the most we both find it fun to have a stupid conversation and roast each other over it.

I knew I wanted to cherish this bond back in the initial stages itself when he was responsible enough to make me study for my semester exams. It was the month of February that made me stress over every passing second for my exams and I rang him up every day and night doing small talk and he always made firm decision to warn me to go study or sometimes would question me of my subject related questions and would never fail to roast me for not being answerable that eventually, I used to turn to go study. Since my exams were in the morning, he would make sure to wake me up early in the morning.

Let me put in a word for his sense of punctuality as I have never seen a person as punctual as him. Though we had time differences according to the countries we lived in, he would never be a second late while ringing up to wake me up. Sometimes he would just ring me up 5 minutes before the usual time because he knew that's how long I would take to wake up after ignoring my phone ringing during the sleep. And he would always know that I'd wake up and go back to sleep, so he'd make sure to call me up every 5 minutes until I get annoyed, wake up and shout at him. He would stay on a video call with me after I'd wake up and revise along with me though I was the one giving the exam. He'd ring me up before leaving to the exam hall and I use to text him right after my exam and he would respond with an "I told you that question was important" statement and I would always wish he wasn't true but somehow, he would always be correct as though he was preparing the question paper for me.

He would study along with me and tell me all his stories and experiences which were like life lessons. My mornings would start, and nights would end with him. There was this one time I was insisting him to listen to a playlist I created, and he wouldn't listen, so I made him listen to it on a video call and we both fell asleep along and when I woke up to his snores, I had a huge smile on my face, and I don't know when was the last time I smiled that wide in my whole life.

Though we stay apart it never feels like we don't live our lives together as we watch stand-up comedy together, cook together, do dishes together, rant together and the best part is his sister helps me roast him. I would rant about everything existing on this earth to him and he always has this subtle way of reacting to each rant that it would always calm me. He'd always explain my rights and wrongs and leave me a choice to decide for myself and this has been the one thing I have craved for the longest time possible "been given a choice". He would not scold me for doing stupid things, instead, he would roast me in a sensible way where I would understand where I went wrong and get an equal scolding for going wrong. He has his days of getting roasted too. It's not like I would let him roast me all the time. The one thing which still amuses me about him is how he has tons of friends and yet each friend of his adores him. Even my best friend who dumped him still adores him for his true identity.

He always knows the state of my mood by the number of memes I send and the number of swears I would use. There are days when we don't text each other a single word, we just stay there in our own lives and we would just video call each other randomly one day, talk for hours about some random topic and then the time just flies. We don't remember what we discussed or small talk we had about, but I do realize I was on a call with this human I never met for about a few hours and I regret wasting my time for so long but really can't deny I have fun. There are these days too when we just stay there on the call but just doing our daily work and just stay silent and observe each other's surroundings as it gives peace we never knew.

Like there are few people whom one feels home with, but Ashish was more like a human with whom you would feel comfortable. Sometimes home feels scary and can be identified as a place where one wouldn't want to belong. But with Ashish, it was like we both belonged to the same home where though home wouldn't comfort things, he would make sure to arrange the home in a manner it would comfort one. He is not a perfect human too but what makes me write about him is the fact that he knows he is not perfect, he acknowledges it, embraces it and inspires one to admire the whole process. But to be honest he's like that annoying sibling you would want to get rid of, but you shouldn't because that's the instinct that keeps holding you back from tossing them into a trash can. I get inspired by a lot of people and I appreciate every human who does that and that's how it goes with Ashish too. He inspires me to be me.

He makes me feel comfortable in my skin, flesh and blood. He encourages me to do the outmost stupid and unnecessary things but also corrects me with his little mocking session we have every single day. He remembers every little detail one mentions, be it the colour of one's shoelace or the deepest secret one shares. The most precious part about the bond I share with him is that I never feel inferior to the world along with him. I don't know if it's the distance that bonded us this way or the particular time we met in or our personalities that could blend this well, but it somehow made me believe that destiny is real. How would a human living 10356 kilometres away with an ocean to cross possibly formed a vibe with another human with the same traits in everything at a very odd period without any possible odds of coming across each other?

I don't think I would ever want to lose what I have with him. He might not be a gem, but he is that crooked discoloured stone among the usual debris that I would want to bury along with my grave. I wish everyone finds an Ashish in their life. Also, the tail doesn't end here. It'll continue as long as one keeps admiring another human.

The Iceman

by Dragon Slayer

So now you know who I am talking about. Where do I start? Where do I end? What am I going to say about him? Every little detail I remember about him is very precious. Our long runs on the roads during the sunsets, our games together, our silly jokes and many more. So, even if I write a book about him, it's not enough. The joy, the laughter, the smiles, the giggles, the care and not but not least the trust that he got my back.

He is not the perfect brother. He never will be. Instead, he was and still is an amazing brother. He is a thin man with dry and messy hair, uncombed for days and carrying a book around with him always and studying by peeping through his glasses as if he is searching for his lost dollar. He has this low pitch voice, and you feel as if he is whispering even when he talks about something.

So, let me start from my first memory of his. This is kind of weird, but I remember him walking around the house without pants during childhood in the house when I can barely get up and stand. He used to take me on a ride on his bicycle. I got the chance to peddle sometimes but mostly he did. We just used to go around the house waving our hands to everyone we see, and we used to laugh our hearts out until my mom came. He used to drive me all around and show me things and tell me about them, which of course I don't remember. That is my first memory of his.

We were together during our schooling. Apparently, I tagged along with him to school because I didn't have anyone else to play with at home and since then we were in the same class until our interests separated us. He is more of logic and scared of blood.

Our schooling was fun. I mean, I never had to think about having a best friend because I had my own brother sitting beside me in the class. I never had to think about anything going the other way. He was always there protecting me. Although I was much more of a troublemaker at school, he was very cool and calm. He used to be like the biggest support at school. It is like having a person telling you that it's alright no matter what happens he is with you till the end of the line. There was a time when they passed a rule at school that we (me and my brother) should not play in the same team. We were "The Brothers of Destruction." Not exactly, but as long as we were together, we never gave up.

There are perks of having your brother in your class as a best friend and there are also many disadvantages. The main thing which is, of course, more irritating is you cannot do the things the way you want. Sometimes I felt like punching him in his perfect teeth.

Many moments come to light when you think about the things you did together. This is the one that keeps reminding me what kind of a person I have to be. One day we were having fun and apparently, I picked up a fight with someone of the same batch. No one stood beside and my brother just stepped in and it's over. I felt really happy and safe at that point or else they would have dismantled me.

One of the best parts of our schooling was our trip where we got a chance to enjoy a lot together and danced all night and discussed random stuff. It was amazing. Although we were together all along, at that moment it felt very pleasant. Long talks and crazy fights and all.

By the end of our schooling, we decided to pursue two different fields. So, our paths diverged from there. Many people told us to take the same field, but it is what it is. One night, we had this serious conversation about life and goals, and I wish I could just go back to that day and slap him in his face because it was amazing.

Even though we were apart, we were in the same college and used to meet during our breaks. The one quality that separates him from everyone I met is his calmness and no matter what happens he stays. I loved going to his classroom and having lunch and meeting his friends. I missed him a lot in the class during that period because it was for the first time we were in different classes. So, it took me a year and a half to adjust to that. I missed him very much, but I didn't tell anybody and not even him but somewhere back in his mind he knew I was missing him so much. After that, it became normal to work on my stuff and focus on my career.

One of the best memories is when I had to figure out my own stuff. I used to sit idle thinking can I do this and that and all the stuff. I fought with my parents too regarding that. At that point, he just stepped in and said: "Leave him alone". He knew I needed my time to get through things. He stood up for me at the time when probably no one believed in me. That's the beauty of the bond we share. It's not the number of times you hung out or the number of times you called him or something, it's believing in each other and supporting each other when no one else does.

Later our paths diverged a lot not only due to our divergent fields but also due to our different opinions on having fun. He likes to play games and watch series a lot and he calls human interaction a curse to his creativity. But, for me, human interaction is a bit essential sometimes, but I do agree with him most of the time.

We have our own plans during weekends. He stays at the hostel, so he comes back every Friday and leaves the next Monday. Basically, we plan how to spend the time and also spend our time doing something. Sometimes we just watch the animated series the whole day. Most of the time we go out for a late show and have some outside food (without telling mom) and come back. This is our routine every Saturday. And sometimes I have to go somewhere on Saturdays but still, I make sure I come back by 10 or 10:30 so that we can hang out.

One of the biggest quests of our times was searching for an old video game (maybe some 90's kids remember it). We spent our whole day searching for it turning everything upside down and we made such a mess. We didn't find it though; all we could find were the cassettes of it. And mom was out of her cool mood and hitting us with shoes was the only thing left to do. But fortunately, it didn't happen, and we didn't clean up the whole mess too.

He really hated me being behind the wheel when we went out. He always says you drive as if you were already dead, and you are not a GHOST RIDER. I don't know but I never hit anything apart from driving classes. He also hates me when I put on an act of some actor and just say the same dialogues in a different tone.

The best things are our secret food missions. We order food on Swiggy or Zomato and one of us has to smuggle the food into the bedroom without anyone noticing it. The food has to come upstairs to the second floor, so one of us has to go and collect it and get it upstairs. And the other one should create a distraction so that mom and dad stay in the dining room until we get it into the living room. Then the second part begins. We switch roles and one has to distract them and the other one should get it into the bedroom. We carried out this mission successfully so many times and I guess we have the best track record if there were any competitions.

Coming to the next part are our games. We play a lot of games together. In fact, once I stole his laptop that he needed for the college to play games as I planned on bunking the next day. He really hated that, but it wasn't important. We play a lot of games and check out new games. Games on our list are counterstrike, Don Bradman cricket, Virtual Tennis, a contest of champions etc. In fact, we feel like we wasted our childhood on games but still no regrets though.

I really hate his long face when I do something to annoy, his games and also his attitude that everything is going to be okay. I like him as much as I hate him. We almost fight every day and it's our way of telling each other that I got your back and I love you.

That's pretty much the story of the ICEMAN and the DRAGON SLAYER.

ACKNOWLEDGEMENTS

Lots of love and gratitude for Kavita Bharadwaj, Shagabandi Mmanish, Y.Vaishnavi, Zeba Farheen and Mrunal Swaroop for always being there and making me feel loved. Thank you for helping me with life and also this book. Throughout years in almost everything I've done, all of you have showered me with love, care and everything else I needed. I can never thank all of you enough!

Most importantly I'd like to thank all of my writers who've shared a beautiful piece of their lives with me as a contribution to fill this book up with enough love. Without all of you, I'd not be able to create this book full of love and warmth!

Sanyogita Bharadwaj
Anthology Editor

Meet the
Co-Authors

Saranya Dhandapani

Saranya is an Engineer by choice and Writer by heart who loves to live life to the fullest. She tries to find muse in every little thing, be it nature, coffee, humans, books. An enthusiastic and loving person who puts her whole heart in anything she sets her mind to and would like to frequently hangout at Crosswords, Cafes and everywhere which is closer to nature.

Anurag Mallick

An occasional writer, Anurag Mallick is a student currently pursuing his master's in Journalism. He aspires to be a sports journo. Otherwise, you can always find him talking about cricket. Pen, camera & cricket defines him the best.

Parasa Meghana

Parasa Meghana is a 22-year-old medical intern pursuing her lifelong dream to be a doctor. Daughter of a single mother, she dreams of dedicating her life to serving people. She is creative, artistic, loves singing and reading fantasy novels. She is a gentle soul that finds beauty in the messiest places.

Laasya Pemmaraju

Laasya Pemmaraju is a law student at Symbiosis Law School, Hyderabad. She likes to engage in niche technological conversations and aspires to practise cyberlaw. Pemmaraju is best known for her discourse at TEDx Silveroaks (2010) on "Conflict Resolution". Her other professional endeavours include debating, delegating, mooting and legal writing.

Rosalind Princess Reshma

Rosalind Princess Reshma is an educator, storyteller, and overthinker who spends her day teaching young, brilliant minds. She holds a bachelor's degree in English Literature, a master's in Applied Linguistics and has an M.Phil. in Translation studies. She has authored two books- Lost Interpretations (2017) and Phantom Listeners (2020).

Raga Lahari

Raga is a 20-year-old aspiring writer offering her readers a unique sense of contentment through her mesmerising ideas, plot twists, and writing style. The characters in her stories can't be helped but loved, for they are made to live not in the story but in the readers' minds.

Madhurya Kommuri

"Love is beyond pain and pleasure, it is beyond one's own self." Madhurya, is an aspiring psychologist by profession and a poet by passion. A perfect imperfection, a beautiful mess is what defines her the best. Bringing out the stories people bury inside with patience and comforting with soothing poetry is her little way of bringing peace to minds and making world a better place for lives.

Shagabandi Mmanish

Shagabandi Mmanish is a young Civil Engineer. He aims to take his business to soaring heights. His interest include debating, public speaking, sketching and fitness towards which he is very much inclined. Writing really isn't his forte but he believes one should try everything life.

Shubha Pai

From acting to writing to singing to dancing to debating to academics, Shubha's interest in everything makes her aspire to be the "Jill of all trades". She holds a degree in Psychology, English and Journalism and is a fan of movies, cricket, psychology, mythology, quantum physics, politics, and DC comics.

Anshika Prem Chhatani

This is Anshika Chhatani, a budding Psychologist during the day and a stargazer for the night. She's also a Succeeding Graphologist and probably never misses a chance to dance! You'll always spot her with a book and coffee (well most of the times, if not always!)

Johnny Pasapala

Johnny Pasapala is a student at Loyola Academy doing a triple major degree in psychology, English, and journalism. He is a feminist, an aspiring journalist/writer, and a fashion enthusiast who likes to sing. He finds his writing inspiration from the moon, his bus rides and Robert frost.

Mansi Gupta

Educator by profession, writer by passion, Mansi has contributed to a few Anthologies and many parenting blogs. A struggling runner who finds sanity in her runs, Mansi believes that the right words will always find the right audience. She spends her day

finding quiet corners to practice Mandalas and pen art, if she is not daydreaming about her short stories. Instagram handle: @mansinipungupta and @letsraisehappykids

Aishwarya K

Aishwarya is a person who believes that everything happens for a reason; it could be a setup for a better future or a punishment for a past mistake. The quest here is to figure out whether it is time to pay or receive payment in life, while using writing as a record of lessons learnt.

Debjyoti Das

Born in Kolkata, Debjyoti has been professionally involved in teaching English Language and Literature. His poems written recently to inspire humanity all over the world during the pandemic crisis have earned recognition from a London based international NGO. He is now writing  in anthologies for several other publications.

Elizabeth Caroline Palaparthi

 A 22-year-old medico, hoping to be a surgeon. She's a fitness enthusiast and a professional swimmer. She's carefree, loves new adventures and new experiences one of which is writing. She loves music, travelling and meeting new people. Above all else she loves her family and friends.

Praneetha Sivalenka

Praneetha Sivalenka is born & brought up in Hyderabad. All that she loves is her family. Her write-ups are in English & Telugu which focus on Equality, youth, and family. DEAR BROTHER, is her debut poem. She started writing articles from the age of fifteen. Her inspiration is her Mom.

Adyasha Pattnaik

Adyasha Pattnaik is currently pursuing her final year of B Pharmacy from GITAM University, Visakhapatnam. She finds writing as a way of escaping into a world of her own. She enjoys reading fiction and poetry the most. She is also currently working on her first book that surrounds the topic of women.

Bhavya Rao

Bhavya is a 20-year-old management student from Hyderabad. She is a curious and confused mind, reading and writing is her escape from reality and calm to her chaotic mind. She tries to flaunt the little things current generation fails to notice like humanity. She connects metaphors to reality.

Dragon Slayer

He is a final year dental student residing at Hyderabad. He is passionate about dentistry and wants to excel in that field. He is into music, sports, and lots of other stuff that he might find interesting. He is also interested in writing but mostly those things stay in his head.

INKFEATHERS PUBLISHING

India's Most Author Friendly Publishing House

Stay updated about latest books, anthologies, events, exclusive offers, contests, product giveaways and other things that we do to support authors.

 Inkfeathers Publishing

 @InkfeathersPublishing

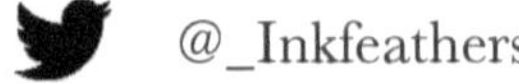 @_Inkfeathers

 @Inkfeathers

 Inkfeathers.com

We'd love to connect with you!